Red is the color of love—and blood.

Mikal never had a home until he found a place at Berith's palace. Now, he's close to the prince and his family—and to Reyni, the prince's personal healer whom Mikal has a crush on. He takes his job as leader of the prince's guards seriously, but sometimes, he's afraid he won't be able to protect the people who matter the most.

Reyni has been head healer for a few years, and he's content with his life, especially after he realizes that his crush on Mikal isn't unrequited after all. The last thing he needs is a war, but unfortunately, that's exactly what he's getting.

Tensions are running high in more ways than Mikal and Reyni could have expected. Can they find their way to each other when their lives are in danger? And if they do, can they build a future together when they don't know if they'll both survive the war looming over them all?

A Demon's Home
Copyright © 2025 Catherine Lievens
ISBN: 978-1-4874-4299-6
Cover art by Martine Jardin

Published by eXtasy Books Inc

Look for us online at:
www.eXtasybooks.com

A Demon's Home
Demons Destinies 6

By

Catherine Lievens

CHAPTER ONE

Mikal didn't usually run from food. He liked food. He liked sweets, salty meals, and snacks. Don't get him started about snacks.

He still couldn't think of anything better to do. He glanced around the dining room, knowing he didn't belong, not in one of these chairs. Sure, he *should* be in the room, but he should be here to protect the people eating, not sitting by their side. What was he supposed to do? Ask his prince how he'd slept last night? Ask the consort what he had planned for the afternoon?

"You know, the bread isn't going to eat you," Mel gently teased.

Mikal swallowed and glanced down at his meal. He hadn't eaten much, and anyone who knew him could tell it was odd. Hell, even the people who didn't know him well could, like Mel.

Mikal hadn't frequented the prince and his consort on a personal level until recently. Berith had always made a point of talking to his guards, but it wasn't like he was best friends with them. Since Mikal had become Lon's second in command, though, he'd been pulled closer to Berith and his family, and now here he was, having lunch with them as if it was completely normal.

"You don't actually have to eat with us if it makes you that uncomfortable," Mel continued, his smile turning into a

1

frown.

The last thing Mikal wanted was to offend the consort. He didn't think Berith would kill him if he did, but Mel was a nice person. He was sweet, and even though he was human, he didn't seem to have problems with demons. Hell, he was in love with one.

Mikal's smile was stiff, but it felt a bit more natural as he turned to the consort. "I'm fine."

"Are you? Because you look like you're about to bolt."

"I'm just not used to eating my meals with you yet. It doesn't feel like I should be."

"Well, considering I trust you with my life, I don't see where else you should be."

"I'm only doing my job," Mikal murmured as he grabbed the bread and his knife to cut a slice.

"A job many people want but few people would be good at," Mel pointed out. "I sleep better at night knowing you're watching over me and my family."

Mikal hadn't come here today expecting to hear that from the consort. He didn't know what to make of it, so he focused on the bread. He cut one slice, then started on another.

The prince's daughter, Cyarea, screeched. Mikal jumped and felt a flash of pain when the knife cut into his finger. He swore and dropped everything to check the cut, from which blood was already spilling.

"Are you all right?" Mel asked as he leaned over the table, reaching for Mikal's hand.

The princess's mother was gently scolding her for making everyone around the table jump. Mikal didn't mind. She was a child, and she should be allowed to act like one, even though one day, she would become their queen.

"I'll be fine. It's just a scratch," he reassured Mel and the others sitting around them. He grabbed his napkin and folded it around his finger. He wasn't about to bleed all over the neat white tablecloth.

Lon's expression told Mikal he wouldn't like what was about to happen, so he wasn't surprised when his friend and boss opened his mouth to suggest he go to the infirmary.

For some reason, Mel seemed delighted by the advice. "Yes, please go to the infirmary. I'd feel better if I knew someone looked at the cut."

"There's no need for me to go. It's barely even bleeding."

"Still. You're protecting the prince's family. I need to be sure that your physical capacity isn't diminished," Lon teased.

It was teasing because Lon knew perfectly well that Mikal could defend the prince and his family, even with a broken arm. It was what they were trained to do—sacrifice their lives for the prince and his family if necessary.

Mikal didn't resent that. He wouldn't have accepted the job if he did. He could never be the prince—too many headaches and attempts on their lives—but he wasn't a fool. Demons needed to be guided. If they were left on their own, they'd kill each other, and the underworld would become an empty space with only memories left. They needed authority, which was where Berith came in.

"Just go to the infirmary," Mel insisted.

Mikal had to resist the urge to roll his eyes at the consort. He knew what the man was doing. "I'm sure the healers have better things to do than to check small cuts."

"And I'm sure that Reyni would be unhappy if he found out that you didn't visit him after you hurt yourself. He's a healer. He'll want to help."

"I doubt he cares. He has many patients, most in worse shape."

"And you're his favorite. He'll be happy to see you." Mel gave Mikal his puppy eyes. "And I'll be relieved to know for sure that nothing's wrong. Do it for me?"

How was Mikal supposed to say no to that? Even if Mel hadn't been the prince's consort, there was no way Mikal could have resisted. The man was too sweet for his own good.

Which was one of the reasons he needed bodyguards.

"Fine," Mikal finally agreed. "I'll go as soon as lunch is over and I find someone to replace me." He wasn't leaving Mel vulnerable.

"You can go now," Lon told him. "I'll keep an eye on Berith and his family. You don't have to worry about them being unprotected."

Not if they were going to be protected by Lon. It was his job as the head of palace security, but more than that, he was one of Berith's closest friends. He'd rather die than allow anything to happen to any of them.

Mikal huffed and got to his feet. "I can see you won't leave me alone until I go. I'll have to finish lunch later."

He thought that maybe this would be enough to make Mel feel guilty and let him stay, but Mel just waved at him. "We'll have the cooks put a plate to the side for you so you can eat once you're done in the infirmary."

The consort was evil, but Mikal wouldn't have it any other way. He might not know what to make of the teasing or of being included in the family he should be protecting, but it felt good. He didn't have family, but he did have friends.

Friends who seemed more than happy to meddle in Mikal's private life.

* * * *

For a moment, when Mikal walked into the infirmary, Reyni couldn't speak. He was socially awkward on the best of days but never as awkward as he was when Mikal was around. How was he supposed to act normally when he couldn't look away from Mikal's hands as he wondered how they would feel around his waist?

There. That was why he was awkward with Mikal. His thoughts went straight down the gutter, even though he tried to stop it, and he got lost in his own head. There was also something about looking Mikal in the eyes when Reyni was wondering how he would feel spread out on top of him, which flustered him every time.

"Mikal," Reyni said after clearing his throat. "To what do I owe the pleasure? Are you feeling ill?"

Reyni loved his job. He especially loved his job now that he was the prince's official healer because it meant he had access to funds his mother had never seen in her life. She'd done her best with what she had, but being a healer was never easy, especially when one didn't have the means to use whatever they could to help their patients. Now that Reyni was Berith's personal healer, though, he made sure there were enough funds allocated to help anyone in need.

Which today seemed to include Mikal.

There was a napkin wrapped around his finger. Reyni reached for it. "Are you in pain? What happened?" he asked as he unwrapped the napkin and threw it into the closest trashcan. He tried to ignore how Mikal's hand felt in his.

"Nothing bad, just the consort and Lon being dramatic. I cut myself during lunch."

"Well, I'll be the judge of how bad it is. Why don't you sit down?" Reyni asked as he gestured at one of the beds.

Berith and his family had private rooms in the infirmary, but Reyni and the other healers took care of everyone else who lived at the palace. That was who the lines of beds in the infirmary were for.

"What have you been up to?" Mikal asked as he obeyed Reyni's order.

Reyni started gathering supplies. He was used to dealing with cuts, burns, and other ailments that happened to the cooks and guards, so he didn't have to think too hard about what he was doing. He moved on autopilot, focusing again only once he was standing in front of Mikal.

"Doing my job," he offered, smiling at Mikal. "You know, the job you're here for."

"I'm here because Lon and Mel are meddlers," Mikal muttered.

His words made Reyni's heart flutter. "Are they? And what are they meddling in?"

"Nothing much. I guess they didn't have anything better to do over lunch."

The cut wasn't bad. In fact, Mikal could have easily taken care of it himself. He was a guard, which meant he was used to cuts and bruises. Reyni didn't take care of every little wound the guards got. If he did, he wouldn't have a life outside the infirmary. Actually, he *didn't* really have a life outside the infirmary. He loved his job, and he felt responsible for the people who needed him.

"There's not much for me to do," he told Mikal. "The cut is shallow and should heal without trouble unless you pick at it. You don't need stitches or anything like that. You don't even need a bandage."

"I know," Mikal said with a sigh. "I tried telling them, but you know how they are."

Reyni did. He interacted with the prince and his family enough to know *exactly* what they were like.

The way they cared about each other was endearing, but what Reyni liked the most was the way they cared about everyone else, too. Mikal was close to them because he was their personal guard and was close to Lon, but still. It would've been easy to dismiss this kind of thing. It wasn't like Mikal was in danger of bleeding out. Mel had still sent Mikal to Reyni. He'd wanted Mikal to see Reyni, even though it wasn't necessary.

6

Fuck. He knew about Reyni's massive crush on Mikal, didn't he?

Reyni was sure he did, even though he'd never had a conversation about Mikal with the consort, even though Mel had tried. Clearly, he'd been so obvious that even the consort had noticed his feelings.

And now, he was meddling.

Mikal slid off the bed. "Thank you."

Reyni hadn't moved away, which meant their bodies were almost plastered against each other. He knew he should move and give Mikal space and allow him to leave, but he was stuck.

He *wanted* to be stuck. He wanted nothing more than for Mikal to drag him into his arms, maybe throw him on one of the beds, and have his way with him. He'd never thought of doing that in the infirmary before, which would have told him how deep his feelings for Mikal were if he hadn't already known.

A door slammed in the distance, making both of them jump. Reyni took a step back, finally allowing Mikal to move. Luckily, it didn't seem like Mikal had noticed anything weird. Maybe he was used to standing so close to his friends. Reyni wouldn't consider himself Mikal's friend, but they were acquaintances, and he felt that Mikal generally enjoyed the time they spent together.

"I'll leave you to your work," Mikal murmured.

"Thank you. And please, feel free to come around for anything."

"Like if another bread knife attacks me?"

"Like that, yes." Happiness bubbled in Reyni's chest, but he pushed it down. Mikal was just being friendly. There was nothing odd about the way they were interacting with each other, and there certainly was nothing that would hint at Mikal being interested in Reyni. No, Reyni's crush was unrequited.

And he was fine with that.

Well, mostly fine. As soon as the infirmary door was closed and Mikal was out of sight, Reyni grabbed his phone. He loved technology. He loved that humans had created it and that demons had stolen it. If it weren't for the humans and their ingenuity, the underworld would still be what it had been decades ago. Now, they had phones and the internet and everything that came with that, and even though a majority of the demons who lived in the underworld still didn't have access to it, Berith was working toward making it more widely available.

"I thought you were at work," Reyni's mother said as she answered.

"I am. You'll never guess who came in."

She sighed. "Oh, I don't know. Mikal?"

"Very funny."

"It *was* him, though, right?"

"Yeah, it was."

"You know, there's an easier way to see Mikal than having to wait for him to get hurt."

"I don't want to hear it." He'd had to listen to his mother rant about the situation enough times. He didn't need a reminder.

"Come on, tell me what happened," his mother gently coaxed.

The infirmary was empty, so Reyni hopped on the same bed where Mikal had sat and proceeded to tell his mother what had happened, even though it hadn't been much.

This was what they did. Reyni told his mother about the cute demon he had a crush on, and she teased him about not doing anything about it.

Rinse and repeat.

CHAPTER TWO

"Your sister was recently seen."

Everyone's attention was on Dimri. Mikal wasn't technically a part of the meeting, even though he had to know what was said in it to protect the palace and its inhabitants, but he was curious. What was Jessamyn up to?

Lucifer groaned. "Of course she was. What is she up to now?"

"Finding allies."

For a moment, Mikal thought Lucifer would hit his forehead on the table. Before, he would've been surprised, but he knew the king of Hell much better now than he could ever have dreamed of. Lucifer had been visiting Berith's palace more and more often since he'd built himself a new palace in the area, bringing with him his consort and chaos. Having him here always gave Mikal a headache, so he was glad he didn't have to deal with him. That was Lon's job.

And the job of Lucifer's consort since he'd been a bodyguard his entire life.

Mikal couldn't imagine anything worse than what had happened to Yakim. He'd been a bodyguard for Berith and his family, a normal person, before he'd fallen in love with Lucifer. Now, he was Lucifer's consort, which meant he had bodyguards himself. He had to dress in expensive and uncomfortable clothes and had to deal with a bunch of idiots day in and day out.

9

To be fair, Mikal had to do the same. Lon never hesitated to give him more tasks, especially now that he was his second in command. At least Mikal didn't have to wear weird clothes and a bunch of jewels he could see Yakim wanted to tear off his body.

"Who?" Berith asked.

Dimri stood next to the door as if he was about to run out. Maybe he was. The spymaster had the tendency to disappear during meetings, and usually, no one even realized he was gone until they looked for him. It was impressive, and Mikal had spent hours trying to keep an eye on the guy just to see if he could catch him sneaking out.

He couldn't.

"Ramiel."

Lucifer groaned again. "I knew he had it in for me. Can we do anything about it? Maybe kill him preventively? No one would care, right?"

"You would," Berith told him. "And while I can't say I'm happy to have to deal with Ramiel, we can't lower ourselves to his level. You have allies now, true allies who will help you."

"I do, but I can't imagine that you want to deal with Ramiel any more than I do."

"I don't, but I'll do what has to be done. What are they up to?" he asked Dimri.

Mikal knew who Ramiel was, even though he'd never met the demon. He hoped he never would. Everything he'd heard about Ramiel indicated that he was a monster, even amongst demons. He was ruthless and bloodthirsty, never hesitated to kill anyone who he felt stood in his way, and that was only the tip of the iceberg. Mikal wasn't surprised that he wanted the throne, and he prayed Ramiel would never get it. Hell was a bad enough place to live in, full of violence and blood. Having someone like Ramiel in charge would make it worse.

"I haven't been there for their meetings, but I can imagine it has something to do with standing up to Lucifer. That's what Jessamyn was aiming at before, and she hasn't given up."

Lucifer leaned back in his chair. "She's never going to get the throne. I won't let her."

"It doesn't mean she's not going to try to take it," Yakim murmured. He pulled on the collar of his shirt and grimaced. "Do I really have to wear these? I'm home."

Lucifer patted Yakim's hand. "You can do whatever you want. You're my consort."

"Yeah, but some of your servants scare me. They forced me into this thing even though I told them I was coming here."

"They want you to make a good impression."

Roque snorted from his spot by the window. "That's not possible."

Yakim turned to glare at him. "What are you saying?"

"You can't make a good impression. You're you."

Yakim started to get up from his chair, but Berith knocked his knuckles on the wooden table, getting everyone's attention.

"We need to focus. Ramiel is dangerous. We don't know what exactly he's planning, but I have no doubt it involves Jessamyn. He might support her taking the throne, or he might be aiming for it himself. Either way, Ramiel isn't just going to stand back and wait. He has to be plotting something, and we need to find out what that something is. We need to be ready when he attacks because he will."

"You think he'd be so stupid?" Lucifer asked.

"He's had his eye on my territory for a long time. He even tried to offer an arranged marriage between him and my daughter when she was born."

Lucifer grimaced. "That sounds horrible. Imagine being married to him."

11

"I doubt she would've lasted more than a few weeks. He would've killed her."

Lucifer's expression was more serious now. "I know you're worried. We all are, including me. The jokes and everything else are just a way to remind myself of what I'm fighting for."

Berith's shoulders slumped. "I know. I'm just convinced Ramiel and Jessamyn are up to something, and I hate not knowing what."

"I'll find out," Dimri promised.

Berith gave him a grateful smile. "Please. But be careful. I don't want to lose anyone to Jessamyn and Ramiel if we can avoid it."

Mikal kept his attention on Dimri so he could catch the moment he snuck out. The others were still talking, but Dimri caught Mikal's eye. He winked, and Mikal prepared himself to finally find out how he did it.

"Mikal, Lon, what do we need to make the palace as safe as possible?" Berith asked.

Mikal turned his attention to the prince for just one second. Lon answered the question so Mikal wouldn't have to. By the time he turned back toward Dimri, though, he was gone.

Mikal swore under his breath. One day, he'd catch the spymaster. He wasn't sure what he'd do when he did, but it was a question of principle by now.

And curiosity.

* * * *

"Save me!" Mel said as he walked into the infirmary.

Reyni would've rolled his eyes, but Mel was the prince's consort. They might be somewhat friendly, but he didn't want the consort to think he was making fun of him.

Even though he deserved to be made fun of, considering how he behaved.

12

"What can I help you with, Consort?"

Mel grimaced and hopped onto one of the beds. "First, you can call me Mel instead of consort. That's my name."

"It might be, but to show respect, I should call you by your title."

"So I should I call you healer?"

Reyni bowed lightly. "You should call me whatever you want."

Mel huffed. "You're no fun. I don't want to call you *healer*. I want to call you Reyni and for you to be my friend."

The reason why Mel wanted that still puzzled Reyni. For some reason, the consort seemed to have taken a shine to him. He always tried talking to him, telling him things Reyni was pretty sure he shouldn't know about the prince, inviting him to dinner and lunch, and even once, to watch one of his classes. Mel might be the prince's consort, but he was also a teacher, and he was still working. No one in his class cared who he was. To the children, he was just Mel, their sweet and lovely teacher.

But Reyni couldn't forget who Mel was. The relationship he had with Berith was nice enough, and Berith was a good ruler, but this was still protocol.

"Please?" Mel asked. "Everyone's in a meeting, and I don't have any more classes today. I just want someone to spend time with."

Reyni pointedly looked around the room. "And you chose to spend time in the infirmary?"

"Not in the infirmary. I chose to spend time with *you*, and you happen to be in the infirmary." He crossed his arms over his chest. "Stop trying to make this harder, and tell me how things are going with Mikal."

Reyni had known that Mel would be trouble from the first time he'd seen him. He'd been right, but the satisfaction of knowing that didn't help him get out of this. "I'm not sure what you're talking about," he said as he moved toward one of the carts he used during emergencies. He'd already restocked it, but he checked everything again just to give himself something to do.

"And I'm not sure who you're trying to fool. Come on. I know you have a crush on Mikal. He has a crush on you, too."

Reyni sucked in a breath. "I don't know what you're talking about." Maybe if he repeated it enough times, Mel would leave him alone.

"Fine. Don't talk to me. I know how you feel, though, and so does anyone with eyes. It's a miracle Mikal hasn't realized it yet, and it worries me. What kind of bodyguard is he when he can't even see what's right in front of his face?"

"Mikal is the best bodyguard you'll ever find," Reyni snapped before he could think better of it.

He pressed his lips together. "I apologize, Consort. I shouldn't have talked to you like that."

"And you shouldn't call me consort, yet here you are, still doing it. You don't even look sorry."

"There's nothing between Mikal and me. We're not even friends. He just visits the infirmary sometimes when he gets banged up, and I take care of him the same way I take care of everyone else in the palace."

Mel sighed. "Fine. I can act as if I believe you for a bit. We're still going to talk eventually, though."

At least he was giving Reyni a heads-up. Hopefully, that meant that Reyni would manage to hide from him the next time he visited.

"In the meantime, what should we do? Are you hungry? Do you want to watch a movie?"

"Nothing I say will change your mind, will it?" Reyni asked, still trying to make sense of the tornado that was Mel.

"Hell, no. I'm not going anywhere, so you better get used to having me in your life."

"I'm a healer. I need to be available in case anyone comes in."

"You're the head healer. Technically, you could get away with only treating Berith and his family."

It was what most of Reyni's predecessors had done. Once they reached the job of head healer, they focused on the prince and did nothing with the rest of their time. Reyni had never been like that, and he hoped he never would be. He was surprised that Mel had noticed, though. "I might get away with it, but it doesn't mean I want to do it."

Mel beamed. "And that's why I like you so much. Come on. Call one of your interns or whatever you call them and put them in charge for a few hours. I need someone to entertain me."

Reyni was pretty sure that Mel was acting like this because he wanted to get to know Reyni. Usually, he was much more subtle, but not today, and Reyni wondered why.

There was only one way to find out.

CHAPTER THREE

Mikal had been sitting at his desk for almost ten minutes when he noticed something moving from the corner of his eye. He sucked in a breath and stayed relaxed, not wanting to alert whoever was there to the fact that he knew they were there. He moved slowly, purposefully, and reached for the knife he always wore at his side.

"There's no need for that," Dimri drawled.

Mikal huffed and dropped his hand. He turned in his chair and glared at the spymaster, wondering where he'd come from. The room had been empty when he'd first arrived. He was sure of it. "What are you doing here?"

"I'm supposed to report."

"Not to me. Lon is in his office." And he was usually the one who talked to Dimri.

Dimri grimaced. "Oh, he is. I went there first, but he's...busy."

Mikal frowned. "I'm sure he would have stopped whatever he's busy with to talk to you. He knows how important this is."

"I wasn't planning on interrupting him and Tobal."

Mikal grimaced, too. He'd walked in on Lon and Tobal so many times he'd lost count. The sight of Lon's naked ass was burned in Mikal's memory. "I see. Is it urgent?"

Dimri sat in front of the desk even though Mikal hadn't told him he could. Mikal didn't take offense. He seldom used his office, so it felt a little odd. His job was in the field, talking to his guards and keeping people safe.

"I have new information," Dimri eventually said. "We're headed toward war."

That wasn't what Mikal had wanted to hear, but he didn't doubt Dimri's words. The spymaster knew what he was talking about. He was good at his job and capable of finding tiny bits of information that would help them—or, in this case, that could put everything in perspective. "Jessamyn?" Mikal asked.

"And Ramiel. They're working together."

"We were aware of that. You know more about their goals?"

Dimri tapped his fingertips on his knee. "Jessamyn is aiming for the throne."

"Nothing new there."

"Ramiel, on the other hand, is coming for Berith. He wants his territory. From what I was able to find out, he and Jessamyn made a deal. She'll take Lucifer's throne, and he'll have Berith's."

This was above Mikal's pay grade, but Dimri wouldn't be telling him this if he didn't trust him to do what needed to be done with this information. "I'll let Lon know. How well are these two working together?"

"They're fine for now, but I don't trust either of them, and I don't think they trust each other. They're focused on their goals, but they wouldn't hesitate to kill each other to get what they want. They're the source of the increased number of fights that have been breaking out in town. They're sending their people to foment disturbances. They probably don't have enough fighters to take us head-on, so they're trying to diminish our numbers from afar, and I'm afraid it's working. I've heard of two guards being killed this week. They tried to stop two fights in taverns, so most people dismissed it, but I think there's more behind all of this."

Mikal nodded. "I'll let Lon know."

"Please do. He's already aware of how serious this is, but I thought I'd confirm it. I'll let him know as soon as I have more information."

He got up, and Mikal briefly wondered if he was going to vanish like he always did. He watched Dimri walk to the door of the office, a bit disappointed to see that everything he was doing was completely normal.

Dimri paused when he was at the door and turned to look at Mikal. "A war is coming, and I don't think we'll be able to avoid it. We'll lose people we care about. We might even die ourselves. We can't be sure who will survive, so maybe we should grab happiness before the fighting starts."

Mikal blinked. "That's a pointed suggestion."

Dimri rolled his eyes. "I wouldn't say it if it weren't pointed. Talk to Reyni. Tell him how you feel."

Mikal would've been embarrassed by the fact that Dimri knew how he felt about Reyni, but he was the spymaster. He knew everything. "I don't know if I can take that risk. Reyni and I are friends."

"Friends who love each other."

"Have you talked to him?"

"I haven't, but I have people everywhere. I know how he feels about you and how you feel about him."

"Don't tell me how he feels."

"Not even if it's good news for you?"

"Not even then. If he wants to tell me, *he* will."

"Or maybe both of you are so worried about ruining things that you're not seeing what's right in front of your eyes."

"Maybe." Mikal trusted Dimri with his life, so he should trust him with this, too, but it was hard. He wanted to believe Dimri and part of him did, but another part was telling him it was impossible.

Why would Reyni want him?

This was Mikal's past talking. He needed to let go of his tribe and everything that had happened with them. He didn't need them, hadn't needed them in years. He had a new family here. *That* was what he should focus on.

He glanced back at the door, not one bit surprised to see that Dimri was gone. He should go and talk to Lon, but if Lon was still busy with Tobal, Mikal didn't want to walk in on that. He should go directly to Berith, and he would have if the prince hadn't been in a meeting with his ministers.

Mikal sighed and looked down at the schedule he'd been working on for the guards. He poked at the sheet of paper for a moment, but he couldn't focus. He couldn't stop thinking about what Dimri had said about talking to Reyni.

He got to his feet. He had no idea what he was doing and what would happen, but he wanted to see Reyni. This could end up either in a disaster or be the best thing in Mikal's life.

Only time would tell which way it would go.

* * * *

Reyni was never very busy, not with patients, anyway. After learning everything he knew from his mother, he'd made a point to have apprentices and teach them as much as he could. There were always at least a few of them around the infirmary, but the patients weren't actually that many. He had a few regulars with illnesses he did his best to cure, which wasn't always possible, but most of the people in the palace were young and healthy.

It was a good thing. It gave him time he could dedicate to his mother's ideas. They both wanted better healthcare for the people who lived outside the palace, and thankfully, Berith was amenable to that. He trusted Reyni with his life and the life of his family. Apparently, he also trusted him with his money, which was a bit of a surprise. Reyni had unlimited funding. He just needed to work on it with Sabin, which he did because he didn't have a head for numbers.

A quick knock on the door made him look up from the document he'd been reading. Berith had signed off on the construction of several medical offices in town. He'd suggested getting Sabin's help to organize everything, but Reyni had thought he could do so on his own.

He couldn't.

"You don't have to knock to come into the infirmary," he said as the door opened and Mikal peeked in.

"I didn't want to bother you if you were working."

"I *am* working."

"If you were with a patient."

"I'm not."

"I can see that. Am I bothering you?"

"Never."

It wasn't a lie. Mikal could never bother Reyni, and Reyni was surprised he'd found the courage to tell him. That was all Mikal would get, though. Reyni wasn't about to confess his feelings for him just because he was cute.

Really cute.

"I was wondering if you had a minute to talk," Mikal said.

"Of course. Did you cut yourself again?"

Mikal shook his head and leaned against the wall. "I was just talking to Dimri."

Reyni nodded. He knew who the spymaster was and even worked on him a few times. He'd never dared ask questions about how Dimri had hurt himself on those occasions, but he'd always been curious. He was curious about Dimri himself, too. Who would want to become a spymaster? How did that work with Dimri's personal life? Did he *have* a personal life?"

Mikal cleared his throat. "He mentioned something about

a higher number of fights in town recently."

Reyni pulled himself out of his thoughts and focused on what Mikal was saying. "He's right."

Mikal cocked his head. "How do you know that?"

"I might look like a sheltered palace healer, but it's not all I am. My mother is a healer in town, and we talk every day. She mentioned having to deal with more fights than usual."

"Damn. I was hoping he was wrong."

Reyni snorted. "Has Dimri ever been wrong?"

"I don't know. He really should be this time, though."

"Can you talk about it?"

Mikal shrugged. "Not in detail. Not because I don't trust you, but it's protocol."

"I'm fine with that."

"Dimri thinks it's a way for Jessamyn and Ramiel to get to us. If they can create a feeling of dissatisfaction and fear, we won't have as many people on the battlefield as we should. It would make it easier for them to defeat us, especially if they continue killing guards."

"But why fighting?"

"At the very least, it's creating unrest, which is the last thing Berith needs."

"How dangerous is it for the people who live in town?"

"It's hard to say, but if things continue the way they are, it would be better if whoever you're thinking about moved temporarily."

That wasn't going to be easy. His mother took her job very seriously, and she wouldn't want to abandon her people. She always said that her place was in town, helping as many demons as she could.

"My mother won't agree," he murmured.

"Maybe move her into the palace so she can be close to you. Surely, she won't disagree with that."

Reyni blinked. "I can't move my parents into the palace."

"Why not? Everyone in the palace is allowed to have a family."

"Yes, but I'm sure someone needs to know about this and approve it."

"That someone can't be me?"

"I know you're Lon's second in command, but it still feels like someone higher up than you should say yes to this."

Mikal huffed. "I see how it is. I'll talk to Lon, then."

"You don't have to."

"I do. You're worried about your parents, as is normal. We both know something bad is coming, and considering who you are, you need to be able to focus. That's not going to happen if you're worried about your parents. Let me talk to Lon, all right? I doubt he'll have a problem with it, but since you don't want to take my word for it, maybe you'll take his."

"I didn't mean to offend you." In fact, that was the last thing Reyni wanted.

Thankfully, Mikal was smiling. "It's fine. You didn't offend me, and I get it. Sometimes, I still can't believe I'm Lon's second in command. It doesn't feel like something that would happen to someone like me."

Reyni frowned. "What do you mean, someone like you?"

"That doesn't matter. Just know that I'll do whatever I can to ensure that your parents are safe. You mentioned that your mother is a healer?"

"She is. She taught me everything she knows."

"Then it would be good to have her with us. She'll be able to help."

Reyni didn't like the thought of needing more healers than the palace already had, but he wasn't an idiot. If this was war, they would need all the healers they could convince to help. Unfortunately, that included his mother.

She wouldn't hesitate. She never did, which was sometimes infuriating, but Reyni had gotten his stubbornness from her. He'd need all of it to convince her to move because she'd want to stay close to her patients. She wouldn't care about helping the prince, but she would want to help Reyni. He had to convince her that he needed her.

That shouldn't be too hard because he did.

* * * *

Mikal wasn't surprised to find out that Reyni came from a family of healers. He *was* surprised to find out that Reyni's mother didn't already work at the palace. Until him, the people who became head healers came from a long line of head healers.

"I don't know how to thank you for this," Reyni murmured as he leaned forward and touched Mikal's arm.

The contact shouldn't be enough to fluster Mikal, but it was. He cleared his throat, trying to think of something to say. "You're welcome. I don't really have a family, but I know how important it is to have them close, and you seem to care about yours."

"I do. What happened to yours?"

This wasn't something Mikal enjoyed talking—or even thinking—about. "They never treated me right, so as soon as I could, I left."

Reyni didn't look surprised. No one would be because, for a lot of demons, children didn't matter. Hell, other demons didn't matter. They were selfish and thought only of themselves, and it wasn't unusual to see packs of children living together on the streets. Berith had always worked hard to ensure they had a safe place to stay, housing them and feeding them, finding them jobs when they were older.

It was how Mikal had ended up at the palace. He hadn't been a child, but he'd been young and lost. He hadn't had a plan. If it weren't for Berith and Lon, he'd probably still be living on the streets. Instead, Lon had taken one look at him and decided he'd be a good guard at the palace. Mikal still didn't know why he'd felt that way, but he'd always be grateful.

"I'm sorry," Reyni murmured. "I'm aware that I'm the weird one when it comes to that. I grew up with two loving parents who I'm still in contact with almost every day."

"I'm happy for you. Everyone should have that."

Unfortunately, that would never happen. Mikal had made his peace with that, so it didn't matter. He was glad Reyni had more support and love than he ever had.

He pushed away from the wall. "Well, I'm sure that by now, Lon and Tobal are done, so I should go and talk to Lon."

Reyni grinned. "Is that why you came here?"

"Yeah. Dimri warned me of what I'd be walking in on, and I decided to give them some time to finish." Mikal shuddered. "You wouldn't believe how many times I walked in on them."

"Oh, I can believe it. I've heard the gossip from the servants."

"Well, if you hear gossip that someone was screaming in the offices, you'll know it was me and that I walked in on something I'll never be able to forget."

Mikal was leaving. Reyni needed to get back to work, but he still wanted to cling to Mikal. Instead, he settled on getting to his feet and touching Mikal's arm again.

Mikal turned and frowned, probably wondering why Reyni was doing that. Initially, Reyni hadn't had a plan, but now, he did, even though it was probably a bad one.

Before he could lose his courage, he leaned forward and kissed Mikal's cheek. He let the touch linger just a bit, silently asking Mikal if it was okay.

Mikal touched the small of Reyni's back. It was light, there and gone, but Reyni had felt it. His entire body flushed, and he had to lean back so he wouldn't do something stupid like kiss Mikal on the lips.

"Thank you for helping me with my parents," he said, firmly staring at Mikal's chest instead of his face.

"It's my pleasure."

Reyni stayed where he was until he heard the infirmary door open and close. Only then did he risk a glance up to find the room was empty except for him. He touched his lips, wondering where he'd found the guts to do that. He had no idea, but he couldn't say he disliked it. Actually, if his guts could make a reappearance the next time he saw Mikal, he'd be grateful.

CHAPTER FOUR

The news of the fighting in the market reached the palace while Mikal was with Berith. A guard came in running, out of breath and with blood on his face. Mikal was instantly alert, stepping forward to stop him before he reached Berith. Mikal recognized him—he knew all of the palace guards because it was his job—but he wouldn't risk it.

"What happened?" he asked as he grabbed Kiani's shoulders.

Kiani was young, but he looked even younger now. His eyes were wide, and he was shaking. There was blood on his cheek. "I was at the market buying a few things when the fight started."

"What fight?"

"I don't know. Initially, it looked like only two people were fighting, but more started joining, and even though I tried to stop them, I couldn't. When I left so I could warn you, there were at least twenty people fighting out there."

"We have a problem," Berith said from behind Mikal.

When Mikal turned, it was to find Berith on his phone. His expression was grim, and he gestured at Mikal to let Kiani go. Mikal wasn't done talking to him, but he had more important things to do.

He turned back to Kiani. "Is there anything else you can tell me?"

"No. There were guards there, and they tried to stop the

fighting, but there were just too many people. They — they killed the guards. I would have died, too, if I hadn't run."

"Don't feel guilty for running. You did what you had to do to save your life and to warn us. Now go to the infirmary, and please let me know if you think of anything else."

Kiani nodded. Mikal wasn't sure he could actually reach the infirmary because his legs were shaking, so he gestured at the two guards standing outside the office.

"One of you take him to the infirmary," he ordered.

Mikal turned back to Berith. He didn't know who Berith was on the phone with, but if he had to guess, it would be Lon. Mikal had his own phone calls to make, so he took out his phone and placed himself so that if anyone walked into the office, he'd intercept them before they could reach Berith.

"I heard about the revolt," the leader of the palace guards, Yuri, said when he answered.

"Is that what we're calling it? The guard who warned me just said it was a fight."

Yuri snorted. "If you want to call it a fight. I'd know how much your guard saw, but it's more than that. Last I heard, there was someone actively pushing these people to fight and demanding to be served Berith's head on a platter."

"That's not going to happen."

"It's not, but it doesn't mean the situation isn't dangerous, especially if it gets out of hand."

"You have everything under control here?"

"Yes. As soon as I heard what was happening, I deployed all the guards. You and Lon don't have to worry about the prince and his family. They'll be safe."

Mikal wasn't going anywhere. He was supposed to spend the day with Berith, anyway. It was a relief to know he'd have backup, though. He was only one demon, no matter how well he was trained.

Everything was a mess after that. People were running

around—guards passing on information because the phones were busy, servants and workers worried about their family members who lived in town, and confused people looking for information. Mikal couldn't do anything for them, unfortunately. He was spending most of his time on his phone and keeping an eye on Berith, who was doing the same.

He'd kept the office door open to see what was happening and to be able to protect Sabin if he needed to, which was why he saw Reyni come in. He quickly ended his phone call, promising to call again as soon as he had more information, and reached Reyni as he was about to enter Berith's office. "Has something happened in the infirmary?" Mikal asked because it was so odd to see Reyni out of the place where he worked.

Reyni shook his head. "Everyone is ready for when the wounded arrive, but that's not why I'm here."

"What is it?" If it was in Mikal's power, he'd give Reyni whatever he asked for.

"My mother has a stall at the market. She and my father go there almost every morning."

Mikal swallowed. He wanted to make promises, but he wouldn't be able to keep them. "I'm sure they're fine."

"Knowing my mother, she's right in the middle of the fight, trying to get to the wounded. I have to go and find her."

"Going out there will get you killed. Everyone knows who you are. Everyone knows you work at the palace."

Reyni frowned. "I thought it was just a regular fight that had gone too far."

"Hopefully, that's all it is, but we can't be sure until we find out what happened. You can't put yourself in danger."

"It's my parents."

"I know, and I promise I'll send someone as soon as I can. You have to trust that your mother knows what she's doing."

"Clearly, you haven't met her."

"No, I haven't, but if she's anything like you, she's scrappy and will come out of this in one piece." That was all they could hope for. Neither Mikal nor Reyni could leave the palace. It was too dangerous.

"Please, Mikal. I need to find my mother and to bring her and my father here."

"I can't spare guards to go with you. I wish I could, but everyone is busy. It's going to have to wait. Besides, I doubt your mother would be happy that you're putting yourself in danger."

Mikal wasn't surprised when Reyni glared at him. He understood where Reyni was coming from and wished he could allow him to leave, or even better, that he could go with him. Instead, they were both stuck in the palace because the prince and his family needed them. It was lucky that Mikal didn't have anyone he cared about. He was able to focus on protecting Berith and keeping everything under control. He couldn't imagine what it was like for people like Reyni, who had family in town and didn't know what was happening to them.

"I promise I'll try to find them as soon as this is over," he said, hoping Reyni would understand.

Reyni put his hands on his hips. "You don't get it. I asked if I could go, but I already knew you'd say no. I'm going anyway, Mikal. I'm not going to abandon my mother."

"Reyni—" Mikal started.

"You can come with me, or you can stay here. Either way, I'm going."

Mikal didn't want to let Reyni go on his own. He didn't want Reyni to risk his life like this. At least if Mikal went with him, he could keep him safe.

But Mikal's duty was to Berith. His job was to stay here and keep the palace and the prince safe. How was he supposed to choose between a job he loved, people he was close to, and

Reyni, who he was falling in love with?

* * * *

Reyni understood where Mikal was coming from. He really did. They had no idea what was happening at the market, but it didn't sound good, so it would be dangerous. Reyni wasn't a fighter, and he wouldn't know what to do if someone attacked him.

That wouldn't be enough to stop him from going. His parents were in danger, and if there was anything he could do to help them, he wanted to do it. He *needed* to do it.

He and Mikal stared at each other. Reyni didn't want to hurt Mikal, but he didn't know what else to do. He'd hoped Mikal would understand.

"Go with him."

Both Reyni and Mikal turned to look at Berith, who was still behind his desk but had put down his phone. He looked tired, and Reyni made a mental note to check in on him once this mess was over. He doubted anything would happen to Berith physically, but it didn't mean he wouldn't need his help.

"I'm sorry?" Mikal asked.

"We both know he's going to go whether we want him to or not. The easiest and safest way to do this is for you to go with him."

It was. Reyni didn't want Mikal to have to choose between him and Berith, but he didn't have to. Berith was telling him to go. It wasn't an order, but Berith was the prince. He didn't need to order people around. They obeyed him even when he didn't.

"My place is with you," Mikal said.

"I'm not going anywhere. I'll stay in my office, and I just hung up with Lon, who told me he's coming here. He'll keep me updated and safe."

Mikal was still visibly hesitant, and while Reyni understood, he needed to stop wasting time. "Thank you," he told Berith.

"Be safe, and bring your parents back to the palace."

"I'll try to convince my mother, but I'm not making any promises."

Berith smiled. "If she's anything like you, I'm not surprised."

Reyni turned to leave. He was scared, but that wouldn't be enough to stop him. He wanted Mikal to come with him, and not only because Mikal would be able to protect him. He didn't want to do this alone.

He would if he had to.

"Wait," Mikal said.

Reyni paused and looked at him. Mikal was still hesitant, but he nodded and turned to Berith. "We'll be back as soon as possible."

"Take as much time as you need. I don't want either of you to do something stupid and get hurt."

"I'll keep Reyni safe, and we'll bring his parents back to the palace. You're sure you'll be okay without me?"

"I am. I'm safe here, so stop worrying about me."

Reyni knew from his job caring for the prince and his family that this was easier said than done. He worried about Berith and his health, even though his job wasn't to protect him.

Mikal nodded and finally moved toward Reyni. He grabbed Reyni's hand and pulled him along, getting him out of the office and down the hallway. For a moment, both of them were silent. They made their way through the palace, and since Mikal was coming and he knew what he was doing, Reyni was happy to let him take the lead.

"You'll do what I tell you when I tell you to do it," Mikal

said once they reached the servants' entrance at the back of the palace.

They had to cross a courtyard to get to the door, which was guarded by two demons. They stood up straighter when they saw Mikal and nodded at him. He nodded back as he waited for Reyni's answer.

"I'll do what you tell me," Reyni said.

Mikal didn't look impressed. "Something tells me that's a lie, but let's go. The sooner we get to your parents, the sooner I can go back to Berith."

Now Reyni felt guilty about pulling Mikal away from his job. "I could go alone," he offered. "I'm sure I can sneak around. People probably won't notice me because I'm no one important."

"You're the prince's healer, so you are, and, more importantly, you *look* important. You might be a healer, but you dress like someone who lives in the palace. People are going to notice that, and I don't want anything to happen to you because of that. You asked me to come with you, and I am. If you're not going to obey my orders, we're not going anywhere."

Reyni was annoyed, but he was also used to obeying orders. It came with living at the palace and working for the prince himself. "I'll do what you tell me to do, I swear."

Mikal gestured to the guards to open the door. The guards didn't hesitate, even though they had to know what was happening out there. They allowed Mikal and Reyni to leave, then closed the door behind them.

The loud thump of the door closing made Reyni jump. It sounded final, as if it would never open again.

He sucked in a breath. He needed to stop overreacting and focus on what he was about to do.

He walked next to Mikal, slightly behind him, as they made their way toward the market. It wasn't far from the palace, and usually, the streets would be full of people headed there, eating food and buying things. There would be families—parents with their children. And while it was normal for a few fights to start, especially near the taverns, they were usually easily dealt with by the guards.

Not this time.

Reyni could hear the fighting before they reached the market. It was loud and mixed with the sound of people screaming and crying. Every time he heard someone, he winced, but he didn't slow down. He didn't think Mikal would allow him to.

Next came the smell of blood. Reyni knew it intimately, but it didn't make it easier to stomach, especially when he knew the circumstances of what was happening. It was mixed with the smell of smoke as if the people fighting had set something on fire. Reyni wouldn't be surprised if they had. It felt like fire went hand in hand with blood and destruction.

He stuck even closer to Mikal now. Their arms brushed as they walked, and Reyni had to resist the urge to snuggle close. He didn't dare call his mother. He didn't want people to find her if she was hiding. He wished he could, though. He needed to know if she and his father were safe.

When he and Mikal reached the marketplace, Mikal gestured at him to stay behind him. Reyni did, slowly following as they finally stepped into the center of the chaos.

Reyni swallowed. He was used to blood, wounds, and even death, but he'd never seen anything like this.

There were bodies everywhere. Some of them were definitely dead, but others were wounded, and his heart went to them. They were calling out for help, trying to drag themselves away, screaming in pain, and his first instinct was to go to them. He stepped forward to do just that, but Mikal grabbed his arm, stopping him.

"I have to do something," Reyni said, even though he knew

Mikal wouldn't allow him anywhere near these people.

"We're here for your mother. I understand how hard this is. I wish I could do something for them, too, but it's too dangerous. The fight isn't over."

It wasn't. Luckily, they'd entered the market from the right side. The fight was located on the other side, and normally, they wouldn't have been able to see much because of the stalls, but they were gone. Most of them were on the ground, but a few were on fire. It still didn't give them a clear view, but it was enough for Reyni to be able to see that a group of at least thirty people were beating the shit out of each other.

He swallowed. "Someone needs to help these people."

"We'll send healers in as soon as it's safe."

"What's the palace doing to stop this?"

Mikal's expression was grim. "Sending guards. Where's your mother's stall?"

Part of Reyni was glad they couldn't stop to help. He wanted to get to his mother, which probably made him a bad healer. He should be thinking about helping people, not telling himself that he needed to check to see if his parents were okay. "I'll show you," he murmured.

Mikal nodded. He stayed close as they walked through the carnage. Several people tried to stop them, and Mikal had to drag Reyni away a few times. Even though Reyni wanted nothing more than to find his parents, he was a healer. He felt the need to help these people, no matter what Mikal had ordered.

They finally reached the side of the market where the healers' stalls were located. His mother's was gone, which wasn't a surprise. What also wasn't a surprise was to find her kneeling next to a demon, pressing something against the demon's stomach. Reyni could see blood, so the demon had probably been stabbed or something similar.

"Mom!" he yelled as he rushed forward.

She turned. There was a streak of blood on her arm, her hair was all over the place, and her lower lip was bleeding, but beyond that, she seemed to be okay.

"Reyni? Come here and help me."

"Your mother is human?" Mikal asked at the same time.

Apparently, Reyni had forgotten to tell him that.

* * * *

Mikal hadn't expected this. How could he have? Reyni looked like a demon. Yes, he also looked a bit human, but a lot of demons did. Most demons had humans in their family tree.

But usually, it wasn't one of their parents.

Mikal had a lot of questions and no time to ask them. He wanted to know why Reyni's mother lived in Hell, how Reyni's parents had met, and how they could still be together. From everything Reyni had said, it sounded like his parents cared about each other. That was the only reason Mikal could think of for a human to move to the underworld permanently. Mel, Berith's consort, had moved because he loved Berith. Clearly, the same went for the woman kneeling next to a groaning demon.

"What's the situation like?" Reyni asked as he knelt next to his mother.

"Stab wound."

Mikal understood the need to help people. The last thing he wanted was to pull Reyni away, but he had to.

"Where's Dad?" Reyni asked as he lifted the fabric his mother had been pressing against the demon's stomach.

"He's trying to find something to help with the wound."

"He needs to get back here. We have to make sure he's safe."

Mikal looked around. He had no idea what Reyni's father looked like, but it wasn't hard to find him. He was poking around the stalls, trying to stay hidden while also looking for things that could be useful.

He was a demon. That wasn't a surprise, considering Reyni's mother was human while Reyni very clearly was not. He had pointed ears and a tail, like Reyni. His skin was a dark pink, and when he straightened, Mikal could see he had completely black eyes, like his son.

He gestured at Reyni's father to come closer. The demon hesitated, but his gaze caught on Reyni and his mother, and that was enough to propel him forward. He stumbled between the stalls, only stopping once he'd reached his family.

Mikal didn't give him time to say anything. He grabbed Reyni's arm and pulled him up, ignoring his protests. "We have to go."

"We can't leave this demon. He's going to die," Reyni argued.

Mikal looked him in the eyes. "It's either him or you. You promised you'd do what I told you."

Reyni stared. Mikal expected him to tell him to fuck off and go back to work. If Reyni did that, Mikal would have to throw him over his shoulder and drag him back to the palace. He didn't care if Reyni hated him after it. He just needed Reyni to be safe.

Reyni's gaze flickered to his mother, then his father. To Mikal's surprise, he nodded. "Let's go."

Mikal turned toward Reyni's father. "I need you to keep an eye on your partner. If she's anything like her son, she's going to try and stop to help half of the people who've been hurt. We need to get back to the palace before the guards get here because it's going to get worse when they do."

The demon nodded. His expression was grim but set, and Mikal wondered how many times he'd had to do something like this. It was clear that just like Reyni, Reyni's mother thought little of her own safety and focused on helping others. It was noble, but it was also foolish, especially in the middle of this kind of situation.

Reyni's father grabbed his partner's shoulder and pulled her away. She squeaked and tried to fight his hold, but he pulled her to her feet. For a moment, they stared each other in the eyes. Reyni's father tilted his head toward Reyni, and that seemed to do it.

Reyni's mother grumbled. "Fine. I'll go, but only to keep Reyni safe."

"Thank you," Reyni murmured.

They'd wasted enough time. Mikal had been keeping an eye on the fighting, and while there were fewer people involved now because several of them had fallen, it was becoming fiercer. Heads were flying — literally — and he could hear the sound of the guards running toward them. They needed to go now if they wanted to be far away from this place before the guards arrived.

He grabbed Reyni's hand and pulled him toward the closest side street. Reyni came without arguing, which was a surprise, but clearly, even he understood how dire the situation was. He let Mikal guide him out of the market and into the streets, following him at every corner. Mikal was careful, but the only demons they encountered were wounded or dead. Several asked for help, and he felt Reyni falter, but he didn't give him the time to do anything about it. He continued pulling him forward until they reached the door of the servant's entrance at the palace.

The two guards reacted on instinct, stepping in their way. It took them a second to recognize Mikal, but when they did, they quickly opened the door. Mikal was relieved when he turned and saw that both of Reyni's parents were there, too. Reyni's mother looked pissed, but she was safe, which was all that mattered.

The guards closed the door behind them. Reyni was safe.

Mikal allowed himself to relax. He had to get back to work, but he would do so more easily now that he knew that Reyni wasn't out there getting himself killed.

He turned toward him. "I have to go."

"I know. I'll stay with my parents and find you once this mess is over, all right?"

"Maybe I'll find you."

Reyni's smile was crooked. "I'll be in the infirmary. I doubt my mother would want to be anywhere else."

"Stay safe, even inside the palace. You never know." Mikal had to resist the urge to kiss Reyni. Now wasn't the moment to do that, even if he'd known how Reyni felt for him—and he didn't.

Turning around and leaving was the hardest thing Mikal could remember doing, but he did it. He had to.

CHAPTER FIVE

Reyni was exhausted. He hadn't gone to bed last night. He hadn't been able to, not once the victims of the fighting had started arriving. Only the worst patients were brought to the palace because that was where the best healers were, but there were still too many of them.

Reyni had slept for a few hours here and there in between taking care of them, and it was starting to get to him. He knew he would have to take a step back soon if he didn't want his exhaustion to start impacting his patients, but for now, he could soldier on, just like his mother was.

He stepped away from one of his new patients and looked around the infirmary. His father was helping as much as he could, but he wasn't a healer. His mother, on the other hand, was with a patient, carefully dressing the wound on the demon's arm—on what remained of it. Unfortunately, they couldn't regrow limbs.

Reyni's father hovered next to her, but he looked up when he heard Reyni move closer. He smiled, and Reyni found himself smiling back.

"How are you doing?" he asked when he reached them.

His father wrapped an arm around his shoulders and pulled him close to kiss his temple. He used to do that a lot when Reyni was a child, and Reyni didn't mind that he continued doing so now that he was an adult. After what had happened yesterday, he understood wanting to comfort and to be reassured. He wanted the same.

His mother finished dressing the wound and stepped away. "We're fine," she reassured Reyni as she patted his cheek. "This place is impressive."

"I owe all of it to Berith."

"Well, of course you do. He wants his family to have the best care possible. It's good of him to open the infirmary to the people who need it."

"He's a good person."

Reyni's mother had been skeptical when Reyni had told her that he was going to work at the palace, but she'd come around. She'd seen what Berith's money could do, and she needed more of it. The entire town did.

"I can't wait to go home," she said with a groan as she stretched.

Reyni frowned. He hadn't yet been able to talk to his parents about what was happening. "You can't go home. It's too dangerous."

His mother rolled her eyes. "We'll be fine. We can defend ourselves, or rather, your father can defend me."

Reyni tilted his chin toward the patient, who was luckily unconscious. "I'm sure they could defend themselves, too, but here they are. Do you really want to put yourself and Dad in trouble?"

"What did you expect? We'll have to go home eventually."

"You could move to the palace."

His mother snorted. "The palace? I'm not going to become a healer for your prince. I don't care who he is. He doesn't need me."

"I'm sure he'd disagree if he could hear you," a voice said. "He always tells me I could find trouble even if I hid from it. I'm pretty sure he's right."

Reyni almost groaned, but he managed to keep the sound in as he turned toward Mel. "What are you doing in the infirmary?" This wasn't the right place for the prince's consort, especially not now that it was full of wounded people.

Mel wasn't looking at Reyni, though. He was staring at Reyni's mother, which wasn't a surprise. Reyni's mother was staring back, even though she'd known that Mel was human. Everyone in town did.

"You're the prince's consort."

Mel looked delighted as he offered her his hand. "I am. You can call me Mel. In fact, *please* call me Mel. I don't want to hear anything about consort and all that."

Reyni's mother stared at Mel's hand for a moment before shaking it. "Angela. I wasn't planning on calling you anything other than your name."

Mel laughed. "Oh, I like you. I've been trying to convince everyone to call me Mel, but they stick to consort."

"That's not a surprise. They like their hierarchy."

"I noticed that. I can see that you're a healer, like Reyni, and you must want to go back to your patients, but I don't think it's safe for anyone to go out there."

"Unless you're going to ask the entire town to move into the palace, someone's going to be in danger."

"I understand. I might be the prince's consort right now, but back in the human world, I was just a guy. I would've been abandoned out there. This town can't afford to lose more healers, though. Several were killed yesterday, and we'd been scrambling to help the people they served. We're thinking about moving all the healers to the palace, where they'll be safe and available for anyone who needs them. They'll also have all the supplies they'll need."

Reyni hadn't known about that, but why should he have? He wasn't the one making these decisions.

Reyni's mother huffed. "Why do you have to use logic on me?"

Mel laughed. "I'm a teacher, and I wish I could go out there and grab all the children. Unfortunately, I can't, not only because I'm the prince's consort. Berith is working hard to find out what's going on and make sure it never happens again, but in the meantime, I would take it as a personal favor if you agreed to move into the palace." His gaze flickered to Reyni's father. "Along with your partner, of course."

Reyni's mother gestured at his father. "This is Harlo."

"The two of you have been together for a long time."

"We have. He's the main reason I'm saying yes to your offer. I need to keep him safe."

Reyni pressed his lips together. He wasn't surprised that Mel had managed to convince his mother to do this when he hadn't. He also wasn't surprised that his mother wanted to protect his father. His father was a demon, but even though his mother was human, she was fierce and could probably kill in a dozen different ways. She was a healer, which was a good thing for the underworld because if she decided to start killing people, the population would be decimated in just a few weeks.

"I'll find you the best rooms," Mel promised. "And I can't wait to talk to you about being a human in the underworld."

Reyni *did* groan this time. His mother and Mel together were a disaster waiting to happen.

* * * *

Mikal wasn't sure what he'd walked in on in the infirmary. He hadn't expected Mel to be there and would need to have a word with his bodyguards because he couldn't see them anywhere. He wasn't surprised that Mel had managed to ditch them, but they needed to do their job. Having Mel roam the palace on his own could be dangerous.

Luckily, Mel had found Reyni and his parents. He was

having a conversation with Reyni's mother, which made sense since the two of them were human and living in the underworld. Mikal was curious to know what they were saying to each other, but it was none of his business, so instead of moving closer so he could hear what was being said, he cleared his throat.

Reyni and his father both looked up, but Mel and Reyni's mother didn't. They were too busy talking. Reyni leaned toward his father to say something. His father nodded and patted Reyni's shoulder, and Reyni moved toward Mikal.

"You look tired," was the first thing Mikal said when Reyni reached him.

Reyni laughed. "I can't believe that's the first thing you said to me today."

"Sorry. I think we all look tired, to be fair."

"Did you manage to get some sleep?"

"I don't know if it counts, but I fell asleep on Berith's couch for about half an hour." Mikal would have to get some rest soon. Luckily, the unrest in the market had been tamed. The palace's cells were full to bursting, and there were still wounded demons coming in, but for now, the town was peaceful. It would take time to clean up and rebuild, and it would take even longer for the people to heal, but the worst was over.

"What about you?" he asked. "I know what you get like when you're working. Have you gotten any rest?"

"Not enough, but I'm pretty sure my mother is going to force me to get some sleep now that the worst patients have been taken care of."

"You should do what she says."

Reyni huffed. "Don't let her hear you say that. She's going to think you're on her side."

"If her side is making sure you're fine, then I am."

Mikal was pretty sure he was being obvious about his

feelings, but he suspected that Reyni was so tired that he wasn't making sense of much right now. That was okay. Mikal didn't want this instant to be the moment in which Reyni realized how much in love he was with him.

"Mikal," Mel said, gesturing at him to come closer. "I need you to take Reyni's parents to one of the guest rooms. They're moving in."

Mikal arched a brow. "Are they?"

"I managed to convince them so Reyni won't ever have to worry about them again. We'll also need more healers in the next few weeks to take care of all the patients, so it's a win-win situation."

"I suppose it is. Can I ask what you're doing alone in the infirmary?"

Mel's cheeks flushed. "I had to make sure that everyone had what they needed."

"And you needed to ditch your bodyguards to do that?"

Reyni's mother put her hands on her hips. "He's the consort. Doesn't that mean he can do what he wants? Are you treating him differently because he's human?"

Mikal's eyebrows shot up. "I'm not treating him any differently than I would any consort. Considering everything that happened yesterday, Mel can't afford to walk around without bodyguards. It would be too easy for someone to snatch him and use him against Berith."

"You're right," Mel quickly said. "And I won't do it again."

Mikal nodded. "Good. Roque is already on his way here."

"He should stay with Berith."

"Do you really think Berith is going to let him do that when you're prancing around the palace on your own? At least he can be sure you won't ditch Roque."

Mel's cheeks were still flushed, but he nodded. "Fine. I'll stay with him."

Mikal bowed lightly. "And I'll take Reyni and his parents

to one of the guest rooms." He turned toward them. "My name is Mikal, and I'm the second in command of palace security. It's a pleasure to officially meet you."

Reyni's father quickly nodded. "Pleasure to meet you. I'm Harlo, Reyni's father."

"Angela," Reyni's mother said. "How close are you to my son?"

Reyni made a strangled sound, but his mother stayed focused on Mikal. "Reyni and I are friends. Now, if you'll follow me?"

Angela huffed and puffed, but she did eventually follow. She, Harlo, and Reyni all did, and Mikal guided them through the palace. Mel hadn't specified which guestroom they needed to be given, so Mikal decided to choose one of the biggest ones. If they were going to stick around, they should be comfortable.

"So," Angela drawled. "Only friends?"

Mikal suppressed the urge to laugh. He was pretty sure Reyni was horrified, but *he* wasn't. In fact, he couldn't wait to hear what Angela said next.

* * * *

Demons couldn't die of embarrassment. Reyni was sure of that because he was a healer, and he knew these things.

Why did it feel like that was happening to him right now, then?

He wished he could get his mother to stop talking, but he'd never been able to do that in all the years he'd lived with her. Even if he did manage to distract her, he was sure she'd find Mikal tomorrow or the day after that and ask all the questions she could think of. Of course, all those questions would involve Reyni in some way.

"Yes, your son and I are friends," Mikal confirmed. "He's

had to patch me up a few times."

"Because you're a guard."

"He's more than a guard," Reyni interjected. "He's second in command when it comes to palace security."

His mother waved his words away. "Which is basically being a guard with more responsibilities."

Mikal laughed. "I suppose it is. Yes, my job is to protect people."

"Including my son?"

"Including your son, especially when he makes bad decisions like throwing himself into a dangerous fight to find his parents."

Why was Mikal doing this to Reyni? Was there a way for Reyni to keep Mikal and his parents away from each other? He'd thought that asking his parents to move to the palace would be a good idea, but now, he had to wonder.

"We'll need to return to our home," Reyni's father quietly said. "I agree that moving here is for the best, but we'll need our things. I'd also like to secure the house if it's at all possible."

Mikal was already nodding. "The city is safe now, so we can go whenever you want. I'll go with you, and I'll ensure we have enough people to pack your things and secure the house."

"We can do that by ourselves," Reyni's mother said, sounding a bit offended.

Reyni knew that Mikal hadn't been trying to say they couldn't. "He's not saying you can't do it on your own," he told his mother. "It would just be faster and safer if we could send someone else to secure the house at the very least."

Mikal nodded. "And if we have professionals do it, we can be sure it'll be done right. But of course, if you'd rather do it on your own, you can. I just know how worried Reyni is about you and how eager he is to have you close."

Reyni's mother huffed. "You know what to say to convince me."

"I assume you're similar to your son, and he wants the people he cares about to be safe. Reyni is going to come to you if you don't agree to move into the palace. It's what you would do, isn't it?"

She wagged her finger. "See, that's why I thought you might be more than friends. You know him very well."

Reyni wasn't sure when that had happened. Yes, he and Mikal were friends, but they'd never been that close. Reyni spent most of his days in the infirmary, while Mikal moved around the palace, going from Berith's office to the training ground to the area where the guards lived. They were both busy, so they didn't have a lot of time to spend together.

Yet Reyni had still managed to fall in love with Mikal. Maybe they did know each other more than mere friends would, after all.

Luckily for him, he didn't have to continue obsessing over this because Mikal stopped in front of a door. They were in the guest quarters, and as far as Reyni knew, most of the rooms here were empty.

Mikal opened the door and stepped aside to let Reyni and his parents in. "If this doesn't work, you just have to tell me, and I'll find something else," he said.

This *would* work. The room was as big as Reyni's, so he knew his mother would have a problem with that. He'd felt the same when he'd first moved there after he'd become head healer. Now, he lived alone in a set of rooms that included a big bedroom, a sitting room, and even an office.

"It's too much," his mother said.

Reyni took her hand. "It's not. There are two of you, and you know how Dad likes having his own space every so often."

"There's a sitting area, as you can see, as well as an office and the bedroom, and, of course, a private bathroom," Mikal quickly said. "You also have access to a private garden. It's not big, but it should be comfortable enough. Now, if you'll excuse me, I have to get back to work. Feel free to contact me if you need anything." He looked at Reyni and winked. "That includes you. No going in town without me."

Reyni nodded because what else could he do? His brain was still trying to make sense of the fact that Mikal had winked at him.

What did it mean?

He watched Mikal walk back into the hallway and close the door behind him. As soon as he was gone, Reyni's mother bumped her shoulder against Reyni's. "Only friends, huh?"

Reyni groaned. This was what he would have to deal with from now on, wasn't it?

CHAPTER SIX

"How are things going in the infirmary?" Berith asked. "I haven't seen or talked to Reyni yet. I know he's busy, so I don't want to bother him."

Mikal almost rolled his eyes at his prince. "You don't want to bother him, so you're asking me?"

Berith smirked. "Who else should I ask? As far as I know, you spend a lot of time there."

"No more time than any other guard."

"Well, any other guard doesn't have a crush on our head healer."

Mikal sighed. "I shouldn't have been so obvious."

"Probably not. It's a miracle that Reyni hasn't realized how you feel about him. That's not what bothers me the most, though."

Mikal hadn't known anything bothered Berith. "What is it?" If there was anything he could do for his prince, he'd do it.

"Well, you're Lon's second in command. Considering your job, I would've thought you would've noticed the way Reyni watches you when you're in the same room. You might have a crush on him, but he's halfway in love with you."

Mikal stared at the prince for a moment, trying to wrap his mind around the fact that Berith was teasing him. He'd become closer to the prince and his family since he'd become Lon's second in command, to the point where they expected him to have his meals with them, but this? He had no idea how to react. He couldn't tell Berith to fuck off because Berith was his prince, but it was clear that Berith was trying to be friendly, and Mikal didn't want to dismiss that.

"Oh, now we're being honest with him about this?" someone said from the corner of the room, making Mikal jump.

He turned to glare at Dimri, who had somehow appeared on the couch. "Where did you come from?"

Dimri arched a brow. "Have you been so busy thinking about Reyni that you didn't notice me coming in?"

"I didn't notice you because you didn't want to be noticed."

"True. Does this conversation mean you finally accepted your feelings for Reyni?"

Mikal pinched the bridge of his nose. "Can we go back to talking about the infirmary? I don't know what's going on with Reyni, and now isn't the best time to talk about feelings."

That was enough to wipe off the smiles on Dimri and Berith's faces. Mikal felt a bit guilty, but they did need to have an important conversation. Normally, Lon would have been here, too, but he had a meeting with the leader of the palace guards. Mikal was in charge of the personal guards who protected the prince and his family, while Uri commanded the other guards in the palace. They needed to coordinate, which wasn't always easy.

"Lon?" Berith asked.

"He should be here any minute," Mikal explained. "But he told me to start without him if his meeting ran long." He looked down at his phone, where he had a list of topics he wanted to mention. "Since you were asking about the infirmary, I'll start with that. Everything's going as smoothly as possible, considering the situation. Reyni has everything in hand, and now that his mother has moved into the palace, they run the infirmary with an iron fist. Reyni has never hesitated to demand more supplies when he needed them, so I don't think we need to worry about that."

"The patients?"

"I emailed you a list with names and other details, but so far, they're doing fairly well. Unfortunately, some of them will need to be supported for the rest of their lives. They lost limbs or, in one case, were paralyzed from the waist down."

Berith sighed and turned to Dimri. "What do you know about this fight? Nothing like this has ever happened before."

Dimri leaned forward. His expression was grim, which was all Mikal needed to know. "That's because usually when there's fighting, it's not organized. You have two or three or even four or five demons fighting, and everyone else is watching. That's easily dealt with by a couple of guards. That's not what happened this time. I looked into every victim of the fight, both dead and alive. Most of the people involved were normal people who were at the market to buy supplies, but about fifteen of them weren't from here. I don't have a lot of information yet, but it seems the visitors had only been in town for a few days, if even that. From what I learned, most of them were killed, while others survived and managed to escape the guards."

"Jessamyn and Ramiel," Berith said.

"I'm inclined to believe that's the case. I have confirmation that they're working together, and as you well know, Ramiel has been coveting your territory for a few decades. My impression is that he's going to use Jessamyn's fight with Lucifer to obtain it."

"Over my dead body," Berith growled.

"I'm afraid that's what he's aiming for. He's not planning to keep you around, Berith. I don't have to ask him to know that his goals are killing you and taking over this territory. Jessamyn will become queen, and they'll all live happily ever after except for us because we'll be dead."

A quick knock on the door interrupted them. Lon strode in, looking tired, but then, everyone did these days. He glanced at them, grimaced, and went to flop on the couch next to Dimri. "I'm almost afraid to ask, but what did I miss?"

"We're in trouble," Dimri told him.

"As if I didn't already know that. Anyone want to fill me in?"

As Dimri started to do just that, Mikal started a new list. His main job was to protect Berith and his family, and to do that, he needed more guards. The problem was that he couldn't just hire anyone to protect the prince's family. He had to find people he trusted with his own life and with Berith's to recommend anyone.

This situation was becoming messier by the day, and Mikal couldn't help but be wary of what things would look like once it was over.

* * * *

"How are you feeling this morning?" Reyni asked as he leaned over the patient in the bed.

It was the demon his mother had been with the other day, the one missing an arm. Reyni hadn't taken care of him, but he'd read his file.

"How do you think I'm feeling?" the demon snapped.

Reyni wasn't surprised or offended at the demon's tone. "I understand this was a life-changing injury for you, and while I won't tell you not to worry, I do want to mention that the palace will be with you. The prince has already announced that he'll ensure that every person wounded or involved in the fighting will be compensated."

The demon's shoulders slumped. "I guess it could be worse."

Reyni wished there was more he could do, but this was something he couldn't heal. He didn't stay with the patient for long, stepping away after he checked his vitals. He glanced around the room, and suddenly, he couldn't be there anymore. It was too much for too long. Normally, he went to his office when he felt like this, but it was too far away, so instead, he opened the door that led into the garden and stepped out. The garden was empty because all the patients were inside, most of them stuck in their beds. Reyni still hid on a stone bench in a corner, needing some time.

He wasn't sure how long he'd been there, breathing and telling himself he'd done everything he could when his mother found him. She hadn't been at the palace earlier, and Reyni had been worried, so he allowed himself to relax now that she was here.

He felt selfish. His parents were both safe, but so many people had lost their lives or loved ones. Reyni felt he shouldn't feel this way, but at the same time, he couldn't avoid it. It was something he'd thought he'd learned to deal with, but this uprising in the market had messed up everyone, including him.

"You need more rest," Reyni's mother said as she sat next to him.

She opened her arms, and even though Reyni was the prince's head healer and a grown adult, he didn't hesitate to snuggle against her. She wrapped her arm around his shoulders and held him close, kissing the top of his head. His position was awkward, and he didn't think he could stay like this for long, but for now, he was happy.

"I'll get rest when everyone's feeling better," he murmured.

"They *are* feeling better. I know you worry about your patients, but you're not doing this on your own. What's going to happen if you collapse from exhaustion?"

Reyni sighed. "Fine. I'll get some rest."

"Good."

"What about you and Dad? I haven't seen you much over the past few days."

"Well, he's been packing the house while I've been talking to my patients. I told them I was moving to the palace and that they were welcome to visit anytime they needed me. I think a few of them were skeptical, but there's nothing I can do about that."

"You're not changing your mind about this, are you?"

She hesitated long enough to scare Reyni, but eventually, she shook her head. "I'm not changing my mind. I want to be close to you, especially after what happened. Besides, I can do more good here, where I have the supplies I need, than I could in our old neighborhood. As long as I have the possibility of going there as often as I need, I'll be fine living here."

"Good."

"Since I'm going to be here, you should tell me what's going on with you and Mikal. I wouldn't want to say something wrong the next time I see him."

Reyni rolled his eyes and pushed away from his mother. "I should've known you were hiding something."

"I'm not the one hiding an entire partner."

"He's not my partner. He's a friend."

"A friend you wouldn't mind having as your partner."

Reyni wasn't going to get out of this conversation. He could try, but he'd gotten his stubbornness from someone, and it wasn't his father. "Fine. I really like him, but that's it."

"That's not an answer. If you like him, what are you planning on doing to make him yours?"

"Nothing. If he was interested in me, he would've said something. We're just friends, and that's fine."

"I didn't think I'd raised a fool. That man does *not* look at you like a friend, Reyni. I understand it's scary, but it doesn't mean you shouldn't do something about it. Even if you don't want to tell him about your feelings, you can ask him about his."

"Not everyone is as brave as you."

Reyni had heard the story many times growing up. His father had visited the human world, and it hadn't been a good trip. Humans up there didn't want demons around, and they weren't shy about it. Reyni didn't blame them.

He'd seen what his mother had to deal with growing up, and while he despised the hate from both sides, he understood being scared and wary of beings you didn't understand.

His father had given up and had been about to return to the underworld when he met his mother. She might have been human, but she hadn't been the least bit intimidated by his father, and she'd introduced herself.

The rest was history, and here Reyni was. His mother had never faltered. She wanted to be by his father's side, and that was what she'd done since the first time they'd met.

"You don't need to be as brave as I was when I met your father. You just have to talk to him."

Reyni nodded, but he already knew he wouldn't. Still, his mother wouldn't let it go until he agreed with her, so this was the easiest way to get her to leave him alone. It wouldn't work forever, but for now, he'd have a bit of respite. He could deal with the gentle scolding he'd get when she realized he'd lied to her later.

CHAPTER SEVEN

"But I wouldn't have to leave the palace, right?" the demon on the other side of the table asked.

Mikal and Uri exchanged a glance. Uri's lips were pressed together, but Mikal couldn't tell if it was because he was trying not to laugh or not to cry. Personally, he'd been resisting tears of frustration since he and Uri had started interviewing the people who'd applied to become palace guards.

He glanced down at his notes for the demon's name. "Well, Jilto, the guards don't actually live at the palace. You'd have to go home eventually."

"What do you mean I wouldn't be living here?"

"We specified that when we put out the request for more guards. Palace guards don't live here. Only the prince's guards do."

Jilto slowly nodded as if he was trying to make sense of the words. Mikal wouldn't be surprised if he was. He didn't look very bright, and that had nothing to do with the fact that his skin was a dark green.

"I can be the prince's guard, then," Jilto offered.

Uri made a strangled sound. Mikal ignored him. "Unfortunately, that's not possible. The prince's guards go through extensive training and are usually picked from the palace guards who've been with us for years." Which was why Mikal and Uri were interviewing prospective palace guards. Mikal needed people to protect Berith and his family, and the easiest way to find them was to pick them from the palace guards. Unfortunately, that meant that Uri wouldn't have enough people, which in turn meant interviewing demons who wanted to work at the palace.

Jilto pouted, something Mikal wouldn't have thought possible with his fangs. "That's too bad. I really wanted to live at the palace."

"You might in a few years if you get promoted." Not that he would be. He wouldn't even become a palace guard.

Mikal was relieved when Jilto finally left. For a moment, both he and Uri were silent. Then, Uri snorted and leaned over the table, hiding his face between his arms as his shoulders shook.

"That wasn't funny," Mikal said.

"I thought it was hilarious."

"Aren't there minimal requirements to become palace guards?"

"Of course there are, but a lot of people come to the interview anyway. I guess they hope they'll be the one exception or something."

"Well, Jilto won't be. That's enough for me. I don't know about you, but as far as I'm concerned, none of these people are what we're looking for."

"I agree."

Mikal rubbed his forehead. So far, the people he and Uri had seen were either idiots, here to take a good look around the palace, or too young and overeager. They might be able to work with the last category, but it meant they might not have enough people to protect the palace until these new guards were trained.

Mikal had a headache by the time he left Uri in his office and headed to the infirmary, needing a painkiller and a dose of Reyni. Mikal would never say that to Reyni's face, but spending time with Reyni helped him relax, which he felt he needed more than painkillers.

The infirmary was quiet when he got there. Most of the patients were sleeping, their bodies working hard to heal. A few of them had visitors and were softly talking, and healers were walking up and down the rows of beds, checking in on everyone.

Since Mikal couldn't see Reyni anywhere, he went to the office. The door was cracked open, so he knocked and waited for Reyni to tell him to come in.

Reyni seemed pleased to see Mikal, but only for a moment. He frowned and was on his feet before Mikal could close the door behind him.

"Why are you here this time? What did you do?" Reyni asked as he ran his hands over Mikal's arms as if to check him for wounds.

"I'm fine. I just have a headache."

For a moment, Reyni looked like it wouldn't be enough to get him to stop checking Mikal, but he relented. "They can be pesky. What were you doing today?"

"Interviewing new guards."

Reyni grimaced and reached over to his desk to grab a small glass vial. "I can see why that would give you a headache. I remember all too well how it was to interview new healers."

He offered the vial to Mikal, who took it. He wasn't one bit surprised to see there were a few pills inside. "Thank you," he said as he shook one out and swallowed it dry.

Reyni grimaced and reached over to his desk again, picking up a glass of water. He offered it to Mikal, who gratefully took it.

"I just don't get it," he explained. "We were specific about what we were looking for, so why did people who had nothing to do with the description show up? And even the people who did match the description didn't fit. There was this one guy who I'm pretty sure wants to become a palace guard so he can beat up people without consequences." Mikal had made a note to look into the guy. There was no way he wasn't violent in his personal life.

The door burst open, causing Mikal to place himself between Reyni and the door. Reyni pushed him away, and when Mikal glanced at him, it was to see he was exasperated.

"What is it now?" he asked his mother.

She had a sly smile on her face that told Mikal that whatever she was planning wouldn't be good.

"I just thought that you and Mikal could go and get something to eat. You both look like you could use a snack."

"We're not children. We don't need you to remind us to get snacks."

"Well, I want a snack from the kitchen. Why don't you go and get it for me?" Her gaze stopped on the vial still in Mikal's hand. "Oh, you're in pain? What happened?"

Mikal was startled when she stepped closer and started touching him the way her son had moments ago. She checked his shoulders and his biceps, then moved down to his elbows.

"He's fine," Reyni muttered. "He just has a headache."

Angela pressed a hand against Mikal's forehead as if checking for fever. "I'm sorry to hear that. You've already taken one of the pills?"

Mikal nodded. He wasn't used to people caring about him so much. His clan certainly hadn't. Even here at the palace, he'd been a palace guard, and most people didn't tend to ask palace guards if they were okay. It hadn't gotten better when he'd become Lon's second in command. He had people who cared for him now, but they didn't care to the point of fussing over him the way Angela was. It was almost as if Mikal was her son, which wasn't something Mikal knew how to deal with.

Reyni grabbed Mikal's arm and pulled him toward the door. "Fine. We'll go and get you a snack. Why don't you sit down and think about what you did?"

Angela laughed as Mikal and Reyni left the infirmary. The sound followed them until they were in the hallway. "What did you mean?" Mikal asked.

Reyni shook his head. "Nothing. It was an inside joke."

Mikal slowly nodded. "I see." He didn't have inside jokes with anyone, least of all his mother. He didn't even know if his mother was alive, and he didn't care.

But Reyni did. He loved his parents, and Mikal was starting to love them, too.

* * * *

Reyni was glad to be away from his mother. He was annoyed that she was meddling, even though he knew she meant well. She'd been poking at him to talk to Mikal since she'd moved to the palace, which, unfortunately, Reyni hadn't thought of before he asked her to. He just wanted his parents close and safe, and he still did.

He just wished his mother would let it go.

"Your mother cares," Mikal said as they walked.

Reyni snorted. "Sometimes, she cares a little too much."

"I don't think it's possible to care too much. I wish I'd had that kind of relationship with my parents."

It wasn't the first time Mikal mentioned not having a happy childhood. Reyni had seen enough of the underworld to know that he was an exception. He had two parents who loved each other and him, who'd raised him and had supported him throughout his life. The same couldn't be said for most demons. "You've never really talked about your family," he said. He was curious, but he wouldn't ask more pointed questions. If Mikal wanted to tell him, he would.

Mikal sighed. "Because there's not much to say. I don't have a family."

"You've mentioned a clan a few times."

"I did grow up in a clan, but I left as soon as I could. It's how I became a palace guard. I moved to the city, lived on the streets for a bit, and Lon found me. He gave me a chance, and I'll always be grateful for that."

"I'm sorry you had to go through that."

Mikal shrugged. "I've made my peace with what happened with my clan." He hesitated. "It's the horns."

Reyni blinked. "I'm sorry?"

Mikal gestured at his head. "The horns. They're short."

That much was true. They were almost invisible, buried in Mikal's black hair, but they were cute. They were light green, like Mikal's skin, and Reyni had thought more than once about what they would feel like if he were to touch them. He didn't dare ask, but that didn't mean he didn't stare when he could get away with it.

"In my clan, females have short horns. Males have longer horns. The longer, the better. I was never respected because of that. My parents tried to hide me and raise me as a female, but I'm not one. I made sure everyone knew that, which made me a problem for the clan. They didn't want other clans to know about me because they viewed me as a weakness."

"That's bullshit. You're far from weak. I mean, you protect the prince."

"I could protect Lucifer himself, but my clan wouldn't care because it still wouldn't make my horns grow."

"Well, I like them."

Mikal blinked, then smiled. "You do?"

"Of course I do. Having horns, short or long, doesn't change the person you are. It doesn't change the fact that you're an exceptional guard and that you chose to protect people for a living. You built yourself a life here. I don't know if your parents would be proud of you if they knew, but I am."

Mikal stopped walking. "You're proud of me?"

It was awkward, but it felt like Mikal needed to hear this. "I am. You just said that you were homeless for a while. Look at where you are now. You live at the palace, are second in command to the head of security, and you're friends with the prince and his family. What's there not to be proud about? As for your horns, well, I don't care that they're short." Without thinking, Reyni reached out and gently touched the right one. "I like them. I think they make you beautiful." He tried to move his hand away, knowing he was invading Mikal's personal space, but Mikal caught his wrist.

"Thank you," he murmured.

"There's no need to thank me. You have nothing to be ashamed of. You have no reason to want to change who you are. Your clan was awful, but you found people who love you for who you are." Including Reyni.

* * * *

Mikal had known that Reyni wouldn't care about his horns. No one here did. Hell, no one in most of the underworld cared. His clan was odd, but he'd left them behind a long time ago, and he'd never regretted it.

He certainly didn't regret it now, with Reyni touching him.

"Thank you," he croaked.

Reyni's cheeks were flushed. Mikal loved it. "You have nothing to thank me for," Reyni insisted.

He gently tugged on his arm so Mikal would let go of his wrist, but Mikal couldn't bring himself to. Instead, he grabbed Reyni's hand and raised it to his cheek. Reyni's eyes widened, but he cupped it and leaned closer.

"You don't have to stop touching me," Mikal murmured.

"I didn't want to invade your personal space," Reyni

murmured back.

"I'd tell you if I didn't like it."

"So you like it when I touch you?"

This was the worst place to have this conversation, but Mikal couldn't stop. He wasn't about to confess that he was in love with Reyni in the middle of a hallway bustling with people, but he could make Reyni understand how important he was to him. "I like it," he confirmed. "Anytime you want to touch me, you don't have to ask."

Reyni chuckled and stroked his thumb over Mikal's cheekbone. "You might regret saying that. What if I never stop touching you?"

"I'd love that."

Reyni swallowed heavily. "Maybe I'll continue touching you, then."

It wasn't the conversation they needed to have, but Mikal was starting to wonder if they actually needed to talk. He hadn't thought that Reyni had feelings for him, but it was clear he'd been blind to the obvious—or at least, that was what people kept telling him. He was pretty sure that Berith and Lon had a bet going over how long it would take Mikal and Reyni to get together. Reyni's mother might want to get in on it, considering she was trying to push them together.

Mikal didn't care about any of that. People could bet on them how much they wanted. It wouldn't change anything—not what he wanted, not who he loved, and not what he hoped his future would be like. Maybe it was time to let go of his fear of rejection. His clan might never have wanted him, but he thought that Reyni did, maybe as much as he wanted Reyni.

CHAPTER EIGHT

"Have you and Uri found what you were looking for, then?" Lon asked.

That was a difficult question to answer. "We have a few names," Mikal said. "It's not what I expected, but we're going to have to make do."

Lon turned to watch the guards. They were training in the courtyard, following Uri's orders while Lon and Mikal watched. Mikal still had a hard time believing that he wasn't one of them. His place wasn't with them anymore.

"I don't like that," Lon said. "We need more people defending Berith and his family."

"That's not going to be a problem. I already handpicked the palace guards who I thought would be good guards for Berith. Hopefully, the ones who remain with the palace guards will be enough to keep the palace safe. With the new recruits, they probably should be able to do that. It all depends on how many people attack."

In Mikal's mind, there was no doubt that the palace would be attacked. He didn't know if Ramiel and Jessamyn would attack head-on, but they didn't need to. This time, the fighting had been at the marketplace. Next time, it would be closer.

"Well, I hope you found some gems," Lon said. "I want the palace to be protected, but I don't want to lose anyone while doing so. We're not here to make widows and orphans."

"We wouldn't be the ones making them," Mikal murmured.

"No. That would be Jessamyn and Ramiel. Still. If we can

avoid anyone dying, we will."

Mikal was somewhat sheltered here at the palace, but he hadn't always been. He knew fighting. He knew pain and blood and death. He'd seen enough of it when he was with his clan, even though they hadn't considered him a fighter. He much preferred to live at the palace and protect people, but if he had to fight and die for his prince, he would.

He just really hoped he wouldn't have to.

Berith was a friend as well as his prince. Mel, Lon, and everyone else were friends, too, maybe even family. There was a risk that someone would die if the palace was attacked, and Mikal had been doing his best not to think too hard about that. He couldn't even consider the possibility of anything happening to Reyni.

He knew Reyni well enough. As a healer, he wanted to be in the middle of things. He might be Berith's personal healer, but that didn't mean he wouldn't want to help anyone who needed him. If the palace was attacked, he'd be where the fight was, pulling people to safety and keeping them alive.

"Is there anything we can do to stop the fight before it finds us?" he asked.

The glance Lon gave him was knowing. "Dimri is working on it. He has a few ideas, but the more information we have before we put them into motion, the better it will be. We won't have a second chance at this."

"We won't need it. We just need to kill Jessamyn and Ramiel."

Lon laughed. "That's easier said than done." He clasped Mikal's shoulder. "But I get where you're coming from. I'm scared, too. Tobal isn't a fighter, even though he can be scrappy. I don't want him to be involved in a fight any more than you want Reyni to be."

"You're in love with Tobal, though."

"Because you're not in love with Reyni? Besides, we both

know that Reyni would throw himself into danger if it meant saving people. Tobal will stay as far away from the fight as he can, though."

That was nothing to be ashamed of. Not everyone was a fighter, and Berith didn't expect them to be. They also needed cooks and bakers and teachers, and Berith was trying to protect all these people. Ramiel and Jessamyn, on the other hand, didn't care about any of them. They only cared about themselves.

"How are things going with Reyni, then?" Lon asked.

They continued walking, reaching the end of the courtyard. "I'm in love with him," Mikal confirmed. "And I think he has feelings for me, too." Reyni had made it obvious the other day when he'd told Mikal that he was proud of him. Mikal had never heard those words from anyone but Lon before, and he'd thought his heart would explode with happiness. He wanted to make Reyni proud, but he knew that Reyni would want him even if he didn't. Mikal's job as Lon's second in command didn't matter to Reyni. He wanted Mikal because of who he was.

"It's about time," Lon teased. "Anyone who sees the two of you together can tell you're in love with each other. You just need the courage to take the first step."

"Sometimes, that first step is the scariest of all."

"I'm not denying that, but taking it could make you the happiest you've ever been. Do you really want to give that up?"

Mikal opened his mouth to say that he didn't, but the words never came out. Someone screamed, and after a few seconds of staring at each other, he and Lon ran.

The scream hadn't come from the guards training behind them. It had come from the gate that opened in the courtyard.

The palace was closed off, especially with the unrest in town, but there were several entrances. There was the main entrance used by Berith and his family, visiting dignitaries, and ministers, or anyone deemed important enough. There was the servants' entrance where the servants used to bring in supplies and come and go. There was a smaller entrance that Berith and his family used when they wanted to sneak out without people being seen, and there was an entrance reserved for the guards. They came and went between the palace and the town so it was easier for them to have a dedicated gate.

That was where the scream had come from.

Mikal didn't hesitate, even though he knew he could be going to his death. He and Lon ran until they reached the gate, but once they were there, it took Mikal a moment to realize what was happening.

People were fighting. The guards were easily identified because they wore their uniforms, so Mikal had no problems doing a quick head count. How had six people with weapons snuck into the gate?

He supposed that the *how* didn't matter right now. What did was that the guards needed help, and he was right there.

He unsheathed his sword from his hip and threw himself into the fight. He and Lon didn't talk, but Lon was next to him, doing the same. Luckily, these attackers had chosen the wrong gate. Mikal wasn't sure how, but they probably hadn't expected to end up in a courtyard full of guards ready to fight to the death to defend their prince.

Mikal ran his sword through the stomach of one of the attackers. The demon's eyes widened, and he reached for the blade, but Mikal didn't give him time. He raised his foot, pressed it next to his sword against the man's stomach, and pushed, freeing his weapon. The demon flopped on the ground, blood already pooling around him.

Movement caught Mikal's attention. He threw himself to the side, but not fast enough. A knife penetrated his thigh, digging itself into his flesh. He swore and raised his sword, stopping the second knife before it could hurt him. The attacker who'd thrown them raised two more knives, but before she could do anything, Lon knocked into her back, sending her stumbling forward. Mikal darted ahead, aiming the tip of his sword at her throat. She looked determined, and Mikal expected her to throw herself at him and not care that he could—and would—kill her.

She didn't get the opportunity to do anything. Lon used the handle of his sword to hit her on the back of the head. She fell to her knees, then forward, hitting the ground with a puff of dust. She wasn't dead, which was a good thing because they needed answers.

"All right?" Lon asked as he neared Mikal.

Mikal looked down at his thigh and winced. "Reyni isn't going to be happy with me."

Lon laughed. "I wish I could be there when he yells at you." He glanced around the courtyard. There hadn't been nearly enough attackers for them to win. With the number of guards both training and guarding the palace, the attackers had already been neutralized. Only two were alive—the demon Lon had knocked out and a male who was on his knees with his hands behind his head.

"Go to the infirmary," Lon ordered. "I'll take care of the clean-up."

"You always keep the easy tasks for yourself."

Lon laughed again. "You know it. You got wounded, and I get all the rewards."

It was good to know they could tease each other even in such a situation, but Mikal's thigh really fucking hurt, so he did as Lon had ordered. He headed to the infirmary.

He wasn't sure he was ready for Reyni's reaction when he saw him.

* * * *

Reyni knew something had happened before he got an official report. That was how gossip worked at the palace, and for once, he was glad for it. That meant he knew to be ready for new patients to arrive, which meant he needed his apprentices to move some of their old ones to make space.

Reyni had been warned, but he still hadn't expected Mikal, of all people, to walk in through the door. He was being supported by a palace guard who looked too young to be doing that job. The palace guard winced every time he and Mikal took a step, but Mikal's expression was stoic. Reyni could tell he was in pain, though. He was pale, and beads of sweat decorated his forehead. He kept biting his lower lip, limping as he moved stiffly. Reyni understood why as soon as he saw Mikal's thigh.

He swore and rushed forward. The palace guard looked alarmed, but he seemed to recognize Reyni's uniform. He let go of Mikal when Reyni reached them, and Reyni grabbed Mikal's shoulder, pressing close. He didn't know what he was about to do until he did it. If he had, he probably would have stopped himself. Instead, he kissed Mikal.

It was awkward and weird because of their position and because Mikal hadn't expected it. Kissing took a certain amount of competence, especially when the person you were kissing had tusks like Mikal did. It didn't matter, though. Reyni just wanted to kiss the demon he was in love with, so he did. He also wanted Mikal to be all right, so he kept the kiss short. When he leaned back, Mikal blinked at him, still pale and sweaty but now also shocked.

"Reyni?"

Reyni grabbed Mikal's arm and gently guided him toward the closest bed. "You threw yourself into danger again."

"I'd say no, but the proof I did is embedded in my thigh,

so I guess I should keep my mouth shut."

Reyni took a step back and bumped into the palace guard. The demon was watching him and Mikal with wide eyes, and he continued doing so even when Reyni waved him off. Reyni rolled his eyes.

"You can go," he told the guard. "I'm sure you have some clean-up to do."

The guard glanced at Mikal for confirmation. Reyni wasn't offended. Technically, Mikal wasn't the guard's boss since he didn't wear the uniform of the prince's guards, but he was still his superior.

"You can go. Tell Lon I'm in the best of hands."

Reyni pulled one of the carts closer and sat down on the stool next to the bed. He leaned close to examine the knife stuck in Mikal's thigh.

"What happened?"

"It seems pretty obvious to me."

Reyni glared up at him. "As obvious as it may be, I want to know what happened."

"One of the attackers threw her knives at me. I caught the second one, but I wasn't fast enough for the first one."

"I can see that. It's pretty deep."

"Yeah, I can feel it is."

The first thing Reyni did was give Mikal painkillers. Mikal tried to argue, but Reyni didn't take no for an answer. Not only did he not want Mikal to be in pain, but it would make it easier for him to remove the knife.

He only had to wait a few moments for the painkillers to take effect. Mikal's body visibly relaxed, and Reyni moved on to his next task.

"I really hope it didn't cut anything important," he muttered. "Do you know how close your femoral artery is?"

"Too close?"

Mikal sounded sheepish, and Reyni wanted to strangle

him. "One cut in your femoral artery, and you'd bleed out."

"You won't let that happen."

He sounded like he had complete faith in Reyni, and Reyni hoped he wouldn't disappoint him.

He worked quickly because he didn't have a choice. After taking all the precautions he needed to take, he slid the knife out. Mikal sucked in a breath and tensed, but he stayed as still as possible. Luckily for him, the knife hadn't hit his artery. There was some bleeding, but Reyni used one of his mother's herbal mixes to stop it. Once that was done, he stitched up the wound.

"That's going to leave a scar."

"That's not a problem unless you don't like scars," Mikal offered.

Was the damn demon flirting while Reyni was stitching up his wound? How could someone be so lovable and infuriating at the same time? "I don't care about scars. I care about you not dying."

Mikal awkwardly patted Reyni's forearm. "I'm not dying. You'll make sure of that."

"I will, just like I'll make sure you don't do anything stupid, like forget to rest and hurt yourself even worse than you already are. You're going to be stuck in here with me for the next few days."

Mikal groaned. "I have work to do."

"You can do all the work you want from one of my beds." If Reyni had to, he'd tie Mikal to the damn thing. Mikal wouldn't get hurt again on his watch.

CHAPTER NINE

Mikal was bored. He'd been in the infirmary for two days, which, as far as he was concerned, meant he was as good as new. He was ready to get back out there, especially because Lon needed his help, but instead, he was stuck in the infirmary.

He glared at an apprentice who walked past the open door of his room. She squeaked and scurried away, making Mikal instantly feel guilty, but not enough to call out for her and apologize.

This was all Reyni's fault.

Mikal crossed his arms over his chest and tilted his head toward the ceiling. Mikal had thought he could convince Reyni to let him go once he'd patched him up, but instead, Reyni had threatened him and even pulled Lon into it. He'd told Lon that Mikal needed rest, and of course, Lon had agreed because Reyni was a healer. Lon had looked like he was about to start laughing when he'd come around a few hours after the attack to tell Mikal he needed to stay in bed and listen to his healer.

Mikal hated him.

He sighed. He didn't actually hate anyone, least of all Reyni and Lon, but he needed something to do before he started screaming.

He looked around. He'd been moved to the area of the infirmary reserved for Berith and his family, as if he was one of them. Hell, Berith himself had visited him the day of the attack to check in on him, which Mikal hadn't expected. He hadn't seen the prince since then, but he hadn't thought he would. Berith and Lon had their hands full, which was why they needed Mikal to get back to work.

The room was empty except for Mikal. The door was open, so he could see that the infirmary was, unfortunately, very busy. Some patients had been here since the attack at the market, and now, there were a few new ones. Several of the guards had been hurt, and Reyni had forced them to stay in the infirmary, too.

The infirmary was busy enough that Mikal would probably be able to sneak out. He imagined that Reyni would hunt his ass all over the palace if he did, but in the meantime, he might have enough time to be productive.

Mikal slid off the bed. He winced because while he was ready to go back to work, his thigh wasn't of the same opinion. It hurt, even with the painkillers Reyni kept throwing down his throat. Mikal would have to deal, though. It wouldn't be the first time he had to work around pain, and probably not the last, either.

He wobbled a bit when he got to his feet and reached for the wall. He paused for a moment, allowing his body to settle. Once he was sure he had his legs under him, he took a step forward, then another.

As expected, it was painful, but he could walk. He wouldn't win a race anytime soon, but he didn't need to, not beyond the race against time before Reyni found him.

He lost miserably.

He wasn't even at the door before Reyni walked in. Reyni stared at the empty bed for a moment, then slowly turned his head toward Mikal, who was hovering next to the door, not moving a muscle. Reyni's eyes narrowed, and Mikal swallowed.

"Do you think that if you don't move, I won't see you?" Reyni asked.

"I can try."

Reyni huffed. He wasn't quite smiling, but Mikal could see he was amused and trying very hard not to show it. "Get your ass back in bed."

"I need to go to work."

"You need to get back to bed." Reyni moved closer and hooked an arm around Mikal's waist. Mikal was relieved to get the weight off his leg, even though he hated himself a bit for that.

"I can't sit here forever," he complained.

"Not forever, just until I say you don't have to anymore." Reyni helped Mikal sit on the edge of the mattress. "Which isn't now." To Mikal's surprise, Reyni leaned forward and kissed him. "I'm not going to allow you to hurt yourself more than you already are. You better get used to that."

He leaned back, but Mikal wanted more than just one kiss, so he hooked his hand around the back of Reyni's neck and pulled him forward again. Reyni laughed and came easily, pressing one hand on Mikal's good thigh and the other on the mattress. He was still smiling when their lips met.

If Mikal had things his way, he'd continue kissing Reyni for the rest of his life. Maybe that was one way for him to stop being bored. If he could convince Reyni to stick around his room for the rest of the day, he could find something entertaining for both of them to do.

But of course, Reyni was a responsible demon, so he wouldn't let that happen. He slowed down the kiss and glared at Mikal. "Don't think you can distract me."

"I'm not trying to distract you."

"It sure felt like it. Seriously, Mikal. What were you thinking? You could have torn your stitches."

Mikal sighed and leaned back against the pillows. "I know. I just can't stand sitting here not doing anything when there's so much to do."

Reyni nodded. "I get it. It's not going to help anyone if you get out of here before you're ready, though. If anything, it's going to make things worse. I'm sure you want to be there for Berith and Lon and everyone else when Jessamyn and Ramiel attack, and you won't be if you don't heal correctly from this wound."

Mikal groaned. "Why do you have to make so much sense?"

"Because I'm smarter than you."

"That's why I love you."

Reyni sucked in a breath. He was staring at Mikal, and Mikal stared right back. He hadn't been planning on saying that, but he didn't regret doing so.

"You love me?" Reyni asked in a quiet voice that didn't sound quite like him. Reyni was usually confident, but not right now.

"I've loved you for a while."

"You never said anything."

"I was afraid it would ruin our friendship."

"You're not afraid anymore?"

Mikal had had time to think about it, so he had an answer ready. "A bit, but I think you feel the same way." All he could do was hope he wasn't wrong. He didn't know what he'd do if he was.

* * * *

Reyni couldn't say he was surprised. Mikal had been obvious about his feelings recently, to the point where Reyni had wondered if they should talk about it. He'd been gearing himself up to do so when Mikal had been wounded, and all of his plans had flown out the window.

They were back.

He'd thought all of this was impossible before, but not

anymore. After their conversation about Mikal's clan, Reyni had been sure of Mikal's feelings almost as much as his own. He didn't know what to do now, though.

He supposed that the first thing was to tell Mikal how he felt about him. "I love you, too," he confessed.

Mikal's smile had been there before, but it stretched his lips now, making him look younger. He still looked tired, probably because he was in pain and wasn't sleeping well, but he'd never looked more beautiful. "Yeah?" he asked.

"How could I not?"

"I don't know. No one has ever really loved me."

"That's because most people are fools. I don't understand why they didn't love you, but I do." And he was glad he wouldn't have to fight anyone to get Mikal's love and attention. He would've lost.

Mikal wiggled to the side of the bed. "Climb up then."

Reyni stared at him. "I'm not climbing into your hospital bed with you. You're not healed enough to do anything."

"Who said I wanted to do anything? I just want to cuddle my new partner."

Reyni's heart raced. "I'm your new partner?"

"What would you prefer I call you? Boyfriend?"

"Partner's fine." Why was Reyni feeling slightly faint? It was normal, wasn't it?

"Well, *partner*, why don't you climb into my bed? I promise I'll keep my hands to myself."

Reyni shouldn't do it, but he really wanted to. Even though Mikal hadn't been badly wounded, Reyni was still worried about him. It could've been much worse, and he didn't know what he would have done if that had been the case. "I don't want to jostle your leg and hurt you."

"You won't. No one knows better than you how to take care of me."

Reyni wasn't sure that was true, but maybe for once, he

could ignore the healer part of himself and focus on the parts that wanted desperately to feel Mikal's arms around him.

He glanced at the door. He couldn't do this in full view of the patients and the apprentices.

He closed the door, sucked in a breath, and sat on the edge of the mattress of Mikal's bed. Mikal would have none of that. He grabbed Reyni's waist and pulled him close, making him squeak in surprise. Reyni glared up at Mikal, but Mikal didn't seem to care. He grinned and settled his arm around Reyni's shoulders, looking happy as a clam.

Reyni was, too. He was careful as he settled against Mikal's chest, then took a deep breath.

He could finally let go. Even though he'd known Mikal was fine since he'd taken the knife out of his thigh himself, part of him had been terrified he would lose Mikal. Instead, he was pressed against him, with Mikal humming and kissing the top of his head.

This was all Reyni had wanted. Now, he had it.

He had Mikal, the demon he'd fallen in love with and had thought would never be his. He didn't know how he'd been so lucky, but now that Mikal was his, he was never letting him go.

"You have to take care of yourself," he murmured against Mikal's chest.

"I'm not good at that, but that's okay because I have you to take care of me now."

Reyni snorted, but Mikal wasn't wrong. He *would* take care of him.

Whether Mikal liked it or not.

CHAPTER TEN

Mikal couldn't stop smiling. He was pretty sure he was freaking out some of the guards, but he didn't care. He was finally back at work. It had been a week since the attack, and even though he knew Reyni wished he could have kept him in the infirmary longer, it was time for him to be productive again. He loved the time he'd had with Reyni, even though Reyni had had to work. But war was brewing, and Mikal needed to protect his people.

He would have done so before because it was his job, but now that he had Reyni to protect, he couldn't just sit on his ass in the infirmary and hope everyone would be okay. He'd grown closer to Lon and even Berith and his family. They weren't just a job anymore.

He walked into Lon's office, doing his best not to limp. He still felt some pain, and Reyni had made him promise to be careful, but he didn't want Lon to treat him with kid gloves. He was here to work, not to sit behind a desk.

Lon was sipping on what Mikal knew was coffee. He went through more cups of the stuff than Mikal could count. Mikal wasn't surprised to see a second cup, and he was grateful for it as he took it and sat down. He took a sip and sighed in pleasure.

"You weren't at breakfast this morning," Lon said.

"I had breakfast with Reyni."

"I take it that things are going well between the two of

you?"

"Better than I could have hoped for."

"It sounds like you finally had *the* talk."

Mikal didn't have a problem admitting that Lon had been right. "We did, and it turns out he's as much in love with me as I am with him."

Lon grinned. "Congratulations. He called me five minutes ago to tell me to keep an eye on you, by the way."

Mikal groaned. "Why?"

"Apparently, you're one of the worst patients he's ever had."

"That can't be right." Reyni hadn't complained when the two of them had made out in Mikal's bed for hours at a time.

"He said something about you not listening to your body and not wanting painkillers. Are you still in pain?"

Mikal was tempted to lie, but he was pretty sure that Lon would see right through him. "If I push myself too hard. As long as I don't spend hours on my feet, I'll be fine. You don't need to confine me to my office or order me to sit down. I know my limits."

"Are you sure about that?"

"I know you're doing this because you care, Lon, but I don't need a babysitter."

"All right. I'm going to trust you with this, but if Reyni has anything to complain about, I'll send him your way."

"It wouldn't be the first time," Mikal muttered.

Lon nodded and picked up his tablet. "Let's get to work, then."

It felt good to settle back into a rhythm. Mikal and Lon spend the morning in the office, going over lists of new recruits and their files to decide who would be doing what. The palace guards Mikal had chosen as Berith's new guards would need to be trained, but he had faith in them. He wouldn't have chosen them if he didn't believe they could do the job. They didn't have a lot of time, but it would have to be enough.

It was lunchtime when someone knocked on the door. Lon had ordered food to be brought up, so Mikal relaxed back in his chair and let Lon get up to open the door.

It wasn't their food. It was Reyni who walked in like he owned the office. "Am I late?" he asked Lon.

"No. Our meal isn't here yet."

Mikal frowned. "What's going on here?"

"I invited Reyni to share lunch with us," Lon explained as he went back to his chair, leaving the door open.

Mikal narrowed his eyes at him. "Why would you do that?"

"Because we're friends," Reyni said as he sat in the empty chair next to Mikal's and leaned over to kiss his cheek. "Lon and I have lunch together at least once a week."

Mikal hadn't known that. "Really?"

"Really," Lon confirmed. "Reyni keeps me informed about what's going on in the infirmary. He hears a lot of gossip there, and it's always good to know what people are talking about. Should I have warned you that he'd be here?"

"No, it's fine." Mikal didn't care that the two of them were friends. He certainly didn't want them to stop being friends. He was just surprised.

"How are you feeling?" Reyni asked. "Any pain? Stiffness?"

Lon snorted, but when Mikal turned to glare at him, his attention was on his phone. Mikal rolled his eyes and turned back to Reyni. "I'm fine. I spent the morning sitting in this chair, so you don't have to worry about me overdoing it."

"I'm still going to. You're not one to sit and let your body heal."

"I took a week off work," Mikal argued.

"You tried to sneak out of the infirmary several times."

"Because I was bored."

"I don't care what you were. You're still healing. You should've listened to me and stayed in bed."

Mikal was very much aware of the fact that Lon was there, listening to every word they were saying. He probably found it hilarious.

Mikal did. He wasn't used to having anyone fussing over him, and it felt good.

They were interrupted by servants bringing in lunch, and Reyni thankfully let it go. Mikal didn't miss the fact that he kept an eye on him during the meal, but it was fine. If this was what Reyni needed to do to be reassured that Mikal would be fine, Mikal wasn't going to stop him. Hard times were coming, and they wouldn't always have a lot of time to spend together.

They were almost done when there was a quick knock on the door. It opened before Lon could tell whoever was there to come in, and Mel walked in, a stormy expression on his face.

"Can you tell Berith that I don't need half a dozen bodyguards following me around the palace? They're scaring people, including my students."

"Do you really think there's anything I can tell Berith that would stop him from being overprotective?" Lon asked.

"You could try." Mel glanced at Mikal and Reyni. "Sorry to interrupt your lunch."

"It's fine," Mikal promised him. It was still strange to talk to the prince's consort as if he was a friend, but he'd been told several times that Mel wouldn't have it any other way, and he didn't want to offend him.

"Berith's stubborn," Reyni said as he leaned forward. "Trust me, I understand everything about having a stubborn partner."

Mel's eyes widened. "Oh?"

Reyni winced. "Please forget I said that."

"No way. Are you telling me that you and Mikal are partners?"

"What if I am?"

Mel squeaked and threw himself at Reyni. Reyni was still in his chair, so he didn't have a choice but to accept Mel's hug. "I am *so* happy for the two of you," Mel said.

It was good to know that Mikal and Reyni had the support of Berith and his family. They didn't need their authorization to be together, but it would have made things much harder if they hadn't been okay with it.

Not that Mikal had expected them to have anything against their relationship. They didn't have a reason not to want Reyni and Mikal to be together. Mikal's clan would have had plenty of things to say about it, but they were long in the past. He had a new family now.

And they were happy for him.

* * * *

Reyni wasn't surprised to see Mel was so happy. He'd been pushing Reyni to talk to Mikal, and Reyni could almost feel the smugness emanating from him. He had no doubt that as soon as Mel caught him alone, he'd want all the details. Reyni wasn't sure how much he wanted to tell him, but he wouldn't have a choice discussing this. For some reason, Mel wanted to be his friend, and Reyni wasn't as opposed to it as he'd been before.

He didn't have many friends. He had his parents, the other healers, and the apprentices, but they weren't exactly friends, no matter how much Reyni cared about them. Mel, on the other hand, fit that word. He was familiar with Reyni in a way Reyni didn't expect from anyone else, and while they weren't best friends yet, it wasn't for lack of trying on Mel's part.

Reyni had tried to resist, but it was pretty useless.

Besides, Reyni liked Mel. He was Berith's consort, but he wasn't intimidating. He didn't think he was better than everyone else, and he treated everyone the same, from Berith to Reyni, to the servants. He was the sweetest person Reyni had ever met, and while that probably had a lot to do with the fact that he was human rather than a demon, what species he was didn't really matter. He was Mel, sweet and gentle and *nice*, and Reyni was a bit emotional at the thought that, of all people, he wanted to be *his* friend.

"Why don't you walk Reyni back to the infirmary?" Lon offered. "Mikal and I still have work to do, and I'm sure the two of you want to spend more time together."

Before, Reyni would have glared at him. He'd found Mel intimidating, even if it was only because of who he was in relation to Berith. He was done with that, though. He still wasn't quite sure what to do or say or what he'd done to deserve Mel's friendship, but he had it, and he wouldn't waste it.

"If that's okay with Reyni," Mel said, looking expectantly at Reyni.

Reyni nodded. "Of course."

The smile Mel gave him was surprised but happy. Reyni felt a pang of guilt at the way he'd pushed Mel away so many times. He hadn't really thought about it before, but Mel didn't have a lot of friends, either. Not only was he human, which meant that a lot of demons would be wary of him, but he was also Berith's consort. Most demons would treat him differently because of that. Reyni had done so until recently.

He got to his feet and patted Mel's arm. "We can go now." He leaned closer to Mikal and kissed his cheek. "I'll see you later, but let me know right away if you feel any pain."

Mikal's expression was fond. "I will, but I don't want you to worry about me the entire day. I'll be fine."

"I'll be the judge of that. Don't tire yourself out, and be mindful of your thigh."

"I will."

Reyni wasn't sure he believed that, but he didn't have a choice. No matter how much he wanted to lock Mikal in the infirmary, far away from trouble and violence, it wasn't his place. Mikal was happiest here, doing his job and helping Lon, and Reyni didn't want to take that from him. He wouldn't be able to, even if he did. Their relationship would only work if they allowed each other to get what they needed, and this was what Mikal needed.

"When did it happen?" Mel asked as soon as he and Reyni were out of the office. "Was it during the week he spent in the infirmary?"

"It was. We had time to talk."

"And you decided to be together."

"We did. He loves me." Sometimes, Reyni still had a hard time believing that, but Mikal never hesitated to tell him how he felt about him.

"Of course he does."

"Was it so obvious?"

"Kind of. It's the way you look at each other, you know? It's the same way I catch Berith looking at me."

Maybe Reyni should have been embarrassed that they'd been so obvious, but he didn't care. He finally had Mikal. He'd be happier if they didn't have to deal with an upcoming war, but they'd get through this, too. He was sure of it.

All of them would survive. Reyni wouldn't have it any other way, and he had faith in the ability of everyone involved. They just needed to survive the next few weeks, and once they were on the other side, they could all be happy.

They *would* be happy.

CHAPTER ELEVEN

It was the first time Reyni had a meal with the prince and his family. He'd been invited because Mikal regularly ate with them, and he wasn't sure how to behave. Yes, he was friends with Mel, and he got along fine with Berith, his daughter, and her mother, but he still felt like he shouldn't be here.

He glanced sideways at Mikal, who was sitting next to him and talking to Tobal, who was on his other side. Both of them looked relaxed, as if they felt completely at ease. They probably did. They'd been sharing meals with the prince for longer than Reyni.

Reyni couldn't deny it did feel like being with family. Berith didn't look like a prince right now. He was sitting next to Mel, allowing his consort to feed him spoonfuls of dessert, rolling his eyes every so often at whatever Lon was telling him. It felt like a normal family meal, a meal Reyni might have with his parents.

Or at least, it felt that way until Dimri suddenly appeared.

Reyni had no idea where the spymaster had come from. He hadn't noticed him sneaking into the room, and from everyone's reaction, he didn't think he was the only one. Mikal looked annoyed and glared at Dimri, But Dimri didn't pay him any attention. He strode toward Lon and Berith, his expression grim.

Reyni put down his spoon and sucked in a breath. This wasn't going to be good, was it? Whatever had happened, it was clear it wasn't good news.

"What is it?" Berith asked when he noticed Dimri.

"They're coming."

For a moment, the room was silent. Reyni didn't know what to say. He was pretty sure that if he opened his mouth, he'd start screaming in terror, and that wasn't something anyone wanted. He needed to focus on what he'd need to do when whoever was coming arrived, not on the fear he felt.

He'd never had to deal with anything like this. He'd been the head healer for a few years, but he'd never lived through a war because Berith's territory was more peaceful than most. Reyni could only imagine how horrible it would be. He'd barely had the opportunity to treat the kind of wounds he would have to deal with, and he could only hope he would be good enough. His people needed him, and he would be there, even though he wasn't sure he could do it.

Berith gestured at one of the empty chairs at the table. Dimri pulled it away and flopped into it, the movement odd to see coming from him. It wasn't like him to move like that, and Reyni leaned forward, unsure if he was ready to listen to what Dimri was about to say.

"Ramiel is sending Jessamyn and a small army of guards," Dimri explained.

"I thought he would be the one attacking us," Lon said.

"He doesn't want to get his hands dirty. Jessamyn thought the same, but he threatened to take back his support, so she doesn't have a choice. He told her that if she won this fight for him, he would fight with her against Lucifer."

"And she believed him?"

"I don't know if she did, but she's coming."

"How many?" Berith asked.

"I don't have exact numbers, but my people are working on it. Several hundred, though."

Reyni leaned back in his chair. His hands shook, so he

pressed them on the table. *Several hundred.* That would mean anything from three hundred to nine hundred. Depending on the exact number, he would have to set things up differently. He needed more details, especially about the possible species of demons who would fight, but he didn't think Dimri had any other information at the moment.

People were going to die. They'd known that since they'd realized they would be attacked, but now that the war was actually starting, it had suddenly become more real.

Reyni didn't want to think about the possibility that Mikal would get hurt. He didn't want any of the people around the table to be involved, but most of them would be. There was a high chance they'd lose someone.

Reyni wasn't sure how they would deal with that. They'd have to find a way, though. There was no escape from this, not when Jessamyn would only back down if she died.

He was already thinking about everything he needed to put together, from the apprentices to the supplies. He'd have to give a list to Lon later. It was ready because he'd been obsessing over it for weeks. He kept the list on his tablet and had tried to ignore it when he wasn't actively working on it, but he'd known he'd have to use it sooner rather than later.

"All right," Berith said as he got to his feet. "Lon, Dimri, in my office. Mikal, keep an eye on everyone. Make sure the family stays in our private wing. It'll be safer for everyone."

There was a stormy expression on Mikal's face. Reyni wasn't sure what to make of it, but he wasn't surprised when Mikal nodded and obeyed Berith's order. Berith left with Lon and Dimri, and Mikal started shepherding everyone out of the room.

Reyni was the last to go. He wasn't part of the family, and he had to get back to the infirmary. He wanted to say goodbye to Mikal first, though.

He was nowhere to be seen, so Reyni waited. Mikal's job

was to ensure that the prince's family was safe, and that was what he was doing. Reyni didn't berate him for that. Right now, he wasn't the center of Mikal's world.

Mikal eventually came back. He still looked worried, but there was something else there. Reyni wasn't sure asking was a good idea, but he did anyway. He wanted Mikal to know he could lean on him. "Everything all right?"

"I don't know."

That wasn't the answer Reyni had expected or hoped for, but he wasn't surprised after the news they'd just gotten.

* * * *

Everything *was* all right at the moment. Mikal had walked Berith's family back to their rooms, ignoring Mel's protests. Mel wanted to stay with Berith, which was understandable, but it wasn't the order Berith had given. As much as Mikal liked the consort, he followed the prince's orders first, the consort's second.

Mikal was frustrated. He understood his role. He was supposed to stick with the prince and his family, to protect them, and not to think about what would happen outside of these walls. There was no way Berith would allow Jessamyn to reach the palace, which meant the fight would happen outside of town and would hopefully stay there.

While Mikal would be here, safe at the palace, playing babysitter and sitting on his ass.

"I just wish there was more I could do," he told Reyni since he genuinely seemed to want to know.

Reyni nodded as if he understood what Mikal was saying. Maybe he did. "You want to be out there to protect your people, but instead, you have to stay here," Reyni said.

So he *did* understand. "Yeah. I know that's my job, but it doesn't feel like I'm doing enough. Besides, my job is also to protect the prince, and I'm not with him." Mikal doubted Berith would allow him to come along when he went into the fight. Lon would go with him. The two of them were best friends and trusted each other to have each other's back. Berith trusted Mikal, too, but they didn't have the same relationship. Besides, he'd want someone he trusted to keep an eye on his consort and his daughter—his heir.

That someone would be Mikal.

"We don't know what will happen," Reyni said as he pressed a hand against Mikal's chest. "What if the fight reaches the palace? We have no idea what Jessamyn and Ramiel have planned, but they won't make this easy on us. Berith needs someone he trusts with his life to protect his family, and that's you. You should be proud of that."

"I *am* proud of it. It doesn't mean I can't wish I could do more."

"No, it doesn't. But if something were to happen to Berith, you'll be protecting the princess. That's a job Berith wouldn't trust many people with."

Mikal sighed. He was aware of that. Cyarea was Berith's world, and not only because she was his heir. "Thank you for reminding me that what I do is important."

Reyni smiled. "Anytime. I know how frustrating it can be to feel like you should do more, but this is all anyone can do. We have to obey the prince's orders, and in your case, his orders will be to protect his people. He's trusting you with his heart."

Mikal hadn't thought of it like that, but it made sense. Berith's heart was his family, and he wouldn't be the person or the prince he was without them. Having Mikal stay with them meant he was trusting him with what was most important to him. Mikal needed to stop thinking about it as if he was being punished. He wasn't.

He was being tasked with the most important job of them all.

Protecting Berith's heart.

Chapter Twelve

The enemy army was approaching. The palace was keeping an eye on them through Dimri and his many spies, as well as through guards and informants.

Waiting for the army to arrive was the worst thing Mikal had ever had to do. He'd rather go back to his clan than have to go through something like this again. Not being able to do anything was incredibly frustrating and made him want to scream.

For now, everyone in town was safe. Jessamyn's army wasn't anywhere near it yet, but it was getting closer every day. It was impossible to hide that fact from the people who lived here, which meant everyone was freaking out and scrambling to do as much as they could to protect themselves and their families. People had started leaving, creating long queues along the roads.

Mikal was freaking out, too, but he was doing his best not to show it to anyone. He couldn't afford for anyone to know he felt that way in his position.

He had plenty of work to focus on that would distract him. He tried not to think about the future that was looming on the horizon, but it wasn't easy when it was all everyone could talk about. Every person he interacted with was stressed, scared, and running around the palace trying to get everything together. The new palace guards always had a stunned expression on their faces, even when they were training. The guards Mikal had added to Berith's protection team were a little better, but not by much. They knew what they risked by accepting their job, and Mikal was satisfied with the fact that none of them had changed their mind, but he also felt guilty.

What if one of them died protecting Berith? It was in the job description, so he normally wouldn't think much about it, but this was the first time these people would have to face something of this magnitude. Mikal wouldn't even be going out there with them. Most of them would be following Berith out in the field, fighting next to him, while Mikal would be here, protecting Berith's family.

He pushed that thought away and focused on the report he was supposed to be reading. He'd already gone through this once. He might hate the fact that he'd be left behind, but he had an important job to do, and he'd do it.

His phone vibrated on his desk, making him jump. He glared at the thing, then snatched it up, wondering who was texting him. Probably Reyni. It was the only way they'd been able to keep in touch regularly since this mess had started. Reyni had just as much work to do as Mikal, but his work was centered on the infirmary. Mikal wasn't even sure he'd been going home to spend the night. He wouldn't be surprised to find out that Reyni slept on one of the beds in the infirmary these days.

Meeting in Berith's office. Now.

Mikal stared at Lon's text for a moment before getting up. His thigh twinged, but he ignored it as he rushed out of his office. Something had to have happened. They regularly had meetings to talk about what was happening, but they were planned. This one wasn't, which meant Lon had news.

Mikal's mind spun as he thought about what might have happened. He didn't think the palace was under attack. People would be panicking if that was the case, and he'd know. No, it was probably Dimri with more information, which was what they needed, but Mikal was still anxious. It was never good when Dimri had information lately. He supposed it was in Dimri's job description—he wasn't Berith's spymaster for nothing.

Reyni was in the hallway outside Sabin's office when Mikal got there. He frowned at his presence but opened his arms so that Reyni could step between them. He kissed Reyni's forehead, happy to have a moment to spend with him. "You were asked to come to the meeting?"

"I got a text," Reyni confirmed. "You know what's going on?"

"I have no idea, but we're about to find out."

Reyni sighed. "I'm not sure I *want* to find out. Every new piece of information these days makes me jumpy."

"How have you been doing?"

Reyni shrugged. "As well as expected. Let's go inside. I want to know what's going on so I can decide if I should freak out or ignore it."

Sabin waved them into Berith's office so they didn't pause. As expected, both Dimri and Lon were already there, talking. Berith was behind his desk, doing something on his phone, but he put it down when he saw them. "There you are. Dimri has something to tell us."

Mikal swallowed. This was it, wasn't it?

"They'll be here tomorrow," Dimri declared.

It was clear that Berith and Lon already knew that. They didn't react the way Reyni did. Reyni gasped and clung to Mikal's hand as if determined not to let him go. He pressed closer, and even though they were working, Mikal didn't hesitate to wrap an arm around his shoulders. He wanted Reyni to know he would always protect him, but could he?

Mikal already knew that Reyni would be in the field when the fighting started. He'd need to be close to Berith in case something happened to him, and, knowing him, he'd be helping as many people as possible, even if they didn't belong to Berith's family. He'd be in more danger than Mikal.

But obsessing over that wouldn't help, which meant Mikal had to stop. It wouldn't do him any good.

"There's no need for anyone to panic," Lon said. "We've all been working toward this. We know what to do."

Reyni laughed. The sound was slightly hysterical, but no one said anything about it. Mikal suspected they all felt that way.

"Knowing what to do doesn't make it easier to do," Reyni said. "But fine. Can I ask why I'm here? I didn't need to be to find out about this. You're going to send a mass text to everyone in the palace, aren't you?"

Lon and Dimri looked at each other. Mikal frowned, knowing they had to have something on their mind. He was pretty sure it couldn't be good.

And it seemed to involve Reyni.

Mikal pulled Reyni closer as Lon started to speak. "The army stopped not far from here. I don't think anyone in town has realized they're here yet, but they're close enough that they'll be here tomorrow."

"You already said they would be."

"Well, Dimri had an idea."

Mikal wanted to ask why they hadn't talked to him first, but he knew why. He and Reyni were together, but Reyni was his own person. Mikal shouldn't be the one making decisions for him. He *wasn't* the one making decisions for him.

"I want to sneak into their encampment," Dimri said. "And poison their water and food."

Mikal stared at him. He wasn't surprised by the plan. It made sense.

Reyni, on the other hand, was shocked. He opened his mouth, then closed it again. "You want my help to kill people?" he asked.

"I don't expect you to go there or anything like that. I just need enough supplies to make it possible."

"You want enough supplies to kill hundreds of people."

"Before they kill us, yes."

Reyni sucked in a breath. "I'm a healer. I don't kill people."

"You won't have to kill them, Reyni. You just have to give me what I need to do it. I understand why you don't want to, but think about it. Think about what will happen if we can't diminish their numbers."

Dimri had found out how many demons would be attacking a few days ago. It was a lot, possibly more than they could handle. The poisoning was a good idea. Mikal didn't think much of it, but he wasn't a healer like Reyni. He had been raised in a clan that didn't think anything of killing people. When it came to saving the people he cared about, he'd do pretty much anything.

Reyni took a moment to answer, but no one pushed him. Mikal knew Reyni wouldn't be forced to do anything he wasn't comfortable with. If he said no, Dimri would find someone else. It would take a little more time, though, which was something they didn't have.

Eventually, Reyni's shoulders slumped, and he sighed. "Fine. Follow me to the infirmary. I'll give you what you need."

Dimri didn't smile. None of them did. They knew many demons would die tomorrow, and no one was looking forward to it. They would do what they needed in order to defend themselves, but they weren't the ones who had started this. No, that was Jessamyn, and the sooner she was out of the picture, the better it would be. Maybe Dimri would manage to poison her, too.

Mikal would always hope.

* * * *

Reyni wasn't happy. He wanted nothing to do with this, but at the same time, he understood why it was necessary.

If fewer demons attacked them, more people on their side would survive. Of course Reyni wanted that. He didn't want to lose any of his friends or other people he knew, and this was a way to level the odds.

But leveling the odds meant he'd be involved in killing people. Could he live with himself after that? Could he really hand over a poison that would be strong enough to kill dozens of demons and continue calling himself a healer?

He supposed he was about to find out. He didn't have a choice, although he knew no one would force him to do it. At least if he was involved, he could choose something that would make death as painless as possible.

These people were coming here to hurt and kill innocents. Hell, they probably wouldn't hesitate to hurt Reyni if they got their hands on him, even though he was a healer and should be left alone. There were no rules that couldn't be broken, or that hadn't already been broken dozens, if not hundreds, of times in the underworld. Usually, people considered healers precious and tried not to hurt them, but he wasn't just a healer. He was Berith's head healer and was in close contact with the prince and his family. He'd be one of the first to go if Jessamyn and Ramiel won this fight.

Reyni swallowed as he walked down the hallway, Dimri following him. He'd be one of the first to go, and he wouldn't be alone. Mikal would be right there with him since he was Lon's second in command. Even if Reyni decided not to do this and to take things how they came, no matter what happened to him, he couldn't do the same when it came to Mikal. He needed to protect him in any way he could.

And this was one of those ways.

He ignored everyone when he reached the infirmary, even

one apprentice who tried talking to him. He went straight to his office. Dimri was silent as always. Reyni closed the door behind them and went to unlock the drawer in which he kept the dangerous mixes and herbs. No one could use them if he didn't hand them over. He didn't keep poisons, but some of the herbs and mixes could be used as poisons. It all depended on quantities.

He took out one of the glass containers and placed it on his desk before closing and locking the drawer again. He stared at the container, telling himself he was doing the right thing.

"How do I use it?" Dimri asked.

He sounded calm and not at all freaked out. He'd probably done this dozens of times. Reyni wanted to ask, but he also didn't want to find out. "You said you wanted to put it into the water?" he asked instead.

"I do. They all need to drink water, and they stopped near a small body of water."

"You realize that if you do that, you'll contaminate the water. No one else will be able to use it."

"We'll put up signs once this is over."

"This is wrong."

Dimri sighed. "I know. I never said it was right or even that I wanted to do it. I just don't think we have a choice. It's them or us, Reyni. We wouldn't be doing this if they weren't about to attack us, but we have every right to defend ourselves. Do you really want to risk something happening to Mikal, or Berith and his family—or your parents? How will you feel if they die and you could have done something to help us win this fight?"

Reyni glared at him. "There's no need to mention my parents. It's obvious I don't want anyone to die."

"And this is the way to do it. It's not going to kill all of them. We'll still have to fight, and fight hard. But it will level the field, which is something we absolutely need."

Reyni sighed. He knew that everything Dimri was saying was true, but he would need some time to wrap his mind around the fact that he'd done it. He wasn't sure what his mother would say if she ever found out, but he had no plans on telling her. "How big is this body of water?" he asked.

"Big enough for several hundred demons to drink there."

"You'll need to use the entire container, then. Dump it into the pond and make sure no one who shouldn't drinks from it."

"What will it do?"

"Kill whoever drinks it." Because their organs would be failing. It wasn't as painless as Reyni wished he could make it, but this was the best he could do, considering how little time he had. "They won't survive the night."

Dimri picked up the container and nodded. "All right."

He hesitated, and Reyni wondered if he was going to try to comfort him again. He wasn't sure what he'd do if that was the case. Maybe scream? It was what he felt like doing. None of this was Dimri's fault, but right now, Reyni didn't like him much.

"You should spend the night with the people you care about. We don't know what will happen tomorrow. No one does."

"That's what I was planning on doing, but thank you for your advice."

Dimri grinned. "I know you're angry at me, and I hope that eventually, we'll be able to get over that. You're doing the right thing, even though it feels like it's not. We both are. I don't know how you managed to grow up so nice and sweet in the underworld, and it's a good thing, but this isn't a nice place, Reyni. You need to accept that."

"I already have."

"I don't know that you have. You're sheltered here at the palace. You don't see the worst the underworld has to offer. I have. Trust me, this is a kindness to the people who will die tonight."

Reyni squeezed his eyes shut and sucked in a breath. Once again, Dimri was right. These demons would fight to death tomorrow if they didn't die tonight.

When he opened his eyes, Dimri was gone. Reyni wasn't sure how he'd left since the door was locked, but he didn't care. He liked Dimri, but right now, the further the demon was away from him, the better.

He decided that the best thing he could do was throw himself into work. He was still dealing with several patients from the market attack and the attack on the palace, and of course, he was obsessively checking everything for tomorrow. He was busy enough that he barely thought about what had happened again until the light coming from the windows faded, and he couldn't avoid it anymore. Thankfully, that was when Mikal found him talking to a patient.

He looked good, even though he was clearly exhausted. They both were. When Mikal opened his arms, Reyni walked into them and pressed his face against Mikal's chest. He inhaled his scent. It felt like this was the last peaceful moment they'd share, and Reyni wasn't ready for that.

"Do you have any plans for tonight?" he asked.

"Just go to bed and sleep as much as I can."

Reyni looked up. "Spend the night with me?"

"Of course."

Mikal made it sound like it was something easy and natural for them, but they weren't there yet, and maybe they would never be. This might be the only night they got to spend together. Reyni hated that they were being rushed into things, that he might never have the opportunity to date Mikal and take things slow, but he'd hate it if something happened to one of them and they hadn't at least had this.

"I'll close up and be right there," Reyni murmured.

Mikal kissed Reyni's forehead and let him go. Reyni had never been so fast to do everything that needed to be done before the infirmary could be settled for the night. He doubted many people would sleep. The apprentices were buzzing with fear and anticipation. The guards were on edge. The servants jumped at every small, unexpected noise.

The silence that fell over the palace as Reyni and Mikal walked to Reyni's rooms was heavy. It had never been quite like this in all the years Reyni had spent at the palace. It was the last night before a battle. Everyone knew what would happen tomorrow. Everyone knew what they would lose. It made Reyni want to scream, but he kept the sound inside, telling himself he could yell as much as he wanted tomorrow on the battlefield.

That was where he would be. Mikal would be at the palace, protecting Mel and the rest of Berith's family. Reyni would be with Berith, ready to help him if he was wounded. They'd already talked, and he'd warned Berith that he wouldn't limit himself to doing that. If Reyni could help others, he would. That would put him in danger, but he'd made his peace with that. He didn't want to die, didn't want to leave all he'd built behind, but this was his job. He helped people.

Even during wars.

He and Mikal stayed silent as they reached his rooms and settled in for the night. They both used the washroom, and by the time Reyni was done and wearing comfortable clothes for the night, Mikal had had someone bring food. Neither of them seemed to be particularly hungry, but Reyni forced himself to eat.

He was jumpy and anxious, and he wasn't sure he'd be able to sleep at all, but he wasn't alone, and that was a relief. When they slid into bed, Mikal instantly pulled him into his arms. It was odd because Reyni couldn't remember the last time he'd slept with someone, but Mikal felt like he belonged. Hopefully, this wouldn't be the only time they did this, but the knowledge that it might be caused him to cling to Mikal. He pressed his face against Mikal's neck, telling himself not to be an idiot and cry. He didn't need to make Mikal feel bad about any of this because there was nothing Mikal or anyone else could do about it.

Reyni wondered if he'd regret not pushing for more than just cuddling under the blankets. He didn't want their first time to be their only time. He didn't want to know what being with Mikal was like if he couldn't have it again, but at the same time, if anything happened to Mikal, would Reyni regret not doing it at least once? Would he regret not knowing what having Mikal's hands on him, maybe Mikal inside him, would feel like?

He didn't know. There was no right answer. There was no *good* answer. He wasn't in the mood to do anything physical that went beyond cuddling and breathing as one. He couldn't stop thinking about tomorrow.

"I can't promise everything will be all right," Mikal murmured as he stroked his hand up and down Reyni's back. "But I can promise you that I'll be careful and that I'll do anything in my power to be alive by the end of tomorrow."

"I promise the same," Reyni murmured back.

Mikal softly snorted. "We both know you'll be right in the middle of things, helping anyone who needs it."

"I will be, but I have you to come back to. That'll make me think twice about doing anything too stupid."

Mikal kissed the top of Reyni's head. "I suppose it's all I can ask for. I'll be here whenever you're done saving the world, Reyni. I'll be waiting for you and praying that you come back to me."

Reyni wanted to promise that he would, but as Mikal had said, they couldn't make promises. They had no idea what would happen tomorrow.

They just knew that it would be bloody and deadly and that if they survived, it would give them nightmares for the rest of their lives.

CHAPTER THIRTEEN

Mikal hadn't wanted to say goodbye to Reyni this morning. It had felt like the last time they'd see each other, and that wasn't something he'd wanted to consider. It had felt like if he clung to Reyni, life would go on as normal.

It wouldn't.

He still didn't know how things had gone with Dimri's plan. His job today was to stay with Mel and the rest of Berith's family, which meant that even though he was being kept up to date with texts and messages, he didn't know everything. People couldn't exactly take their time to inform him of what was happening when they had to focus on staying alive.

Hopefully, Dimri's plan had worked, and they'd managed to kill or at least put out of commission a lot of demons fighting for Jessamyn. Even if they had, though, they'd still have plenty more demons to fight.

Mikal had faith in Berith and their people. He'd overseen the training of many of the guards at the palace, and while he had nothing to do with Berith's army, he was sure they were just as well trained.

Mikal paused in front of the window and peered out. From where he was, he could see the army in the distance, but he couldn't tell what was happening. He was only slightly surprised that everyone else in the room was avoiding the windows. They probably didn't want to watch what was going on since there was nothing they could do to help.

There was nothing Mikal could do to help, either. He stepped away from the window and started pacing again, his thoughts going to Reyni.

He was out there. He wasn't fighting, but he'd still be way too close to the action for Mikal to feel comfortable. Knowing him, he'd throw himself into danger without thinking twice about it just because someone needed his help. It was something Mikal would have found endearing any other time, but right now, it made him want to drag Reyni home and lock him up in the infirmary.

"Could you stop pacing?" Mel asked in a tone that was harsher than usual.

Mikal obeyed instantly. "Sorry."

Mel sighed and rubbed his face. He was wearing human clothing—a pair of shorts and a t-shirt—and looked more rumpled than usual. His hair was standing on end because he'd been running his fingers through it, and he was pale. If Mikal hadn't known what was happening, he would have been worried. He *was* worried, but not for Mel, not right now.

"I'm sorry," Mel murmured. "I didn't mean to snap at you. I know you're as worried as I am because Reyni is with Berith. It's not fair for me to treat you like that."

"It's fine," Mikal told him. It really was. Right now, Mel wasn't just Berith's consort. He was his partner, and he worried as such.

"It's really not."

Mel glanced around the room. Berith's daughter was playing with her mother in a corner. She wasn't worried, but then, she probably didn't fully understand what was happening. Aloise was trying to focus on her, but she kept glancing in the direction of the window.

They were all on edge.

"Do you think it's already started?" Mel asked. "I'd check through the window, but I don't know if I can do it."

"You can't see anything, anyway. I'm sure it has. Berith wouldn't waste time. He wants this to be over as soon as possible, and the best way to do that is to attack."

Mel nodded. "Do you think Dimri's plan worked?"

Mikal leaned against the wall by the window and did his best not to glance outside. The only thing he'd be able to see was people moving around, which was what he'd seen earlier, too. They were too far away to be able to make sense of anything.

"He went there himself, so I think it worked," Mikal said. "Dimri would know exactly where to put the poison, and since Reyni provided it, it'll have been lethal."

"I hate that we had to put Reyni in that position. I know he didn't like it."

Reyni and Mel hadn't seen each other that day. Reyni had rushed to the infirmary after saying goodbye to Mikal, and Mikal had come straight here. No one had wanted to sit down to have breakfast.

It was a little sad to think that they hadn't known that the last time they'd had breakfast together might truly have been their last. What if someone didn't survive? What if the next time they all sat together, there were empty chairs at the table?

"He didn't like it," Mikal confirmed. "But he knows it was necessary."

"Still. As a healer, I imagine he had a hard time dealing with it."

"He did. I stayed with him last night, so I made sure he knew that whatever happened wasn't his fault, but it does hurt him to know that he's helped kill people instead of saving them. He understands it was necessary, though."

Mel didn't tease Mikal for having spent the night with Reyni. He probably wasn't even surprised to find out they had. "I'll have to talk to him once he comes home."

Mikal prayed he *would* come home, him and everyone else they cared about. "I'm sure he'll be happy to see you."

A loud explosion propelled Mikal forward before he could think about moving. He grabbed Mel and pulled him close, then moved toward Cyarea. She was in her mother's arms, and Mikal was glad to know he wouldn't be the only one protecting the heir and the consort. Aloise could be lethal, even though she looked dainty.

"What is it?" Mel asked.

That was when the screaming started. Mikal's stomach dropped, and he exchanged a glance with the two guards standing by the door. He'd wanted to have Roque here, but the bodyguard was with Berith, where he should be. These guards might not be the best of the best, but they were good, and they would defend Mel to death.

"I don't know," he told Mel. "But if I have to guess, the palace is under attack."

The sound of screaming was loud. Mikal could also hear people running, and as desperately as he wanted to go and see what was happening, he couldn't. He couldn't leave Mel's side.

He took out his phone to check if anyone had sent him a message, but there was nothing new. Uri was no doubt busy defending the palace, so he wouldn't have the opportunity to warn Mikal about anything.

Mikal didn't need to be warned. He knew what was happening and what his job was. If the attackers managed to get past the palace guards, they'd have to face Mikal and his guards.

A loud pounding on the door made Mel jump and squeak. He pressed closer to Mikal as if he was afraid that Mikal would leave him behind.

"Who is it?" Mikal called out.

"Uri sent me," a voice answered. "The palace is under attack."

Mikal sucked in a breath. He'd known that, of course. He could hear it. The screams that had started after the explosion had never stopped. If anything, they had become more numerous, a sure sign that more people were getting hurt.

"Do we know anything?" he called out.

"I counted dozens of attackers before I was sent here," the guard said.

"Do you have to go back?"

"No. Uri told me to stay here and protect the consort and the heir."

"I'll leave you to that, then. Keep me updated if you can. Right now, you're my eyes outside of this room." Them and the guards outside the door.

The voice chuckled. Mikal couldn't tell if it was male or female, but it didn't matter, and he didn't care. "I'll be your eyes wherever you need them to be," the guard promised.

It wasn't as much as Mikal needed, but it was better than nothing. Hopefully, it would be enough to keep the people in this room safe.

Mikal glanced out the window. He still couldn't see what was happening any better, and he had other things to focus on right now, but he couldn't help but wonder what Reyni was doing and if he was hurt.

* * * *

"Keep that pressed on," Reyni ordered the wide-eyed demon. "I'm serious. If you stop pressing it against the wound, you risk bleeding out."

The demon nodded. Reyni wasn't sure that would be enough—he didn't think it would be—but he had no other choice. He couldn't stop to cauterize the wound and stitch the demon back together. He had dozens, if not more, other patients to check.

Reyni pushed away from the demon and gestured at one of his apprentices to help. She rushed forward, but her expression was grim. She had to know that there was only a slim chance the demon would survive. That wouldn't stop her from trying, just like it wouldn't stop Reyni.

It wouldn't be enough.

Reyni continued moving forward. His hands were dirty with blood, no matter how many times he cleaned them. He didn't have water, so he had to use a piece of fabric, but the thing was almost as soaked as Reyni's clothes.

He wore the black healers' uniform, which identified him as such to both sides. In theory, it meant that no one would try to hurt him, but while he trusted Berith's people not to, he couldn't say the same for their enemies. Something told him they wouldn't care that he was a healer, just that he was on Berith's side. That meant he had to be *extremely* careful as he moved through the battlefield.

He wasn't right in the middle of the fight. There, he'd be useless and, even worse, a hindrance. He was a few feet behind, helping the demons who had fallen. Sometimes, they managed to drag themselves to him, while other times, he had to move closer to the battle and drag them out. They were all lucky that the poison had taken out so many enemies because there would have been many more casualties otherwise.

For now, he hadn't been hurt, but he wouldn't be surprised if he was eventually. It might not even be by people actively trying to kill him. There was so much happening around them that even though his uniform was obvious, he could easily get hit by a stray sword or knife.

Someone cried out to his left, and he rushed that way. He understood the problem before he even knelt next to the demon. She was stretched out on her back, holding what remained of her arm against her chest. Blood bubbled from her mouth, painting her chin and chest. There was a wide cut in her neck. It was a miracle that she hadn't died.

Yet.

Reyni had a choice to make. If they'd been in the infirmary, he would have done everything in his power to save her. It would have been desperate then, too, but here? It would be impossible. She probably wouldn't even survive the trek back to the palace, let alone Reyni trying to help her. His heart cried for her, but there truly was nothing he could do to help. She would die, no matter what he came up with.

He opened the bag that hung by his side and dug through it. So far, he hadn't had to make this decision, but he did now, and it made him want to throw up. He was a healer. His job was to heal and help people, and instead, he found himself looking through his supplies for a drug that would kill the demon bleeding out in front of him.

"Help me," she croaked.

Reyni's eyes burned with tears, but he refused to shed them as he nodded. He was pretty sure she knew what was happening, but he didn't want her to be afraid. He didn't want her to be alone. "I'm going to help you," he promised.

"It hurts."

"I'm going to give you something for the pain, all right? You just have to swallow."

He finally found the vial. He and his mother had worked on this together. His mother had been worried and wary, but when he'd explained why he'd need it, she had understood. He was glad she wasn't here, though. She would never have been able to do this, even though she would've known it was the best thing to do. No, she was safe in the infirmary back at the palace, ready to help the wounded who were no doubt already arriving. Reyni had to deal with this on his own, and that was fine. It was his job.

He uncorked the vial and hovered the stopper above the woman's mouth. He gently used the fingers of his other hand to open her lips and drop one drop of the liquid into her mouth.

She licked her lips. The blood coming out of the wound in her neck was slowing down, and her eyes were hazy. She wouldn't survive for much longer, and while what Reyni had just done might have been deemed unnecessary by other people, he wanted her to have a quick and painless death. If that was the only thing he could do for her, he'd do it.

"How are you feeling?" he asked in a whisper as he put away the vial. He suspected he would have to use it many more times today. It broke his heart, but he told himself that he just had to get through today. He could break down when he went back to the palace. He could cry in his bathtub and take all the time he needed once this was over.

"It doesn't hurt anymore," the demon murmured. "That's good, right?"

"Very good," Reyni promised. "The medicine is working."

"I'm tired," she said. She'd been clutching the stump of her wounded arm against her chest, but her body relaxed now, and it slipped away.

"Then you should close your eyes and rest. Someone will be with you to help you move soon, all right?"

"Yeah, all right."

Reyni gently touched her shoulder. She blinked her eyes open for a moment, and he pressed his hand down, smiling at her.

"Thank you," she whispered.

"Just rest," he whispered back because he didn't know what else to say.

She nodded, and Reyni watched her as her breathing slowed. He wasn't sure how much time passed, but it couldn't have been more than a few minutes before she stopped breathing entirely. A sob escaped his throat, and he let go of the demon's shoulder to press his hand against his mouth. This time, he couldn't keep the tears inside, and they rolled down his cheeks.

He'd just killed someone. He'd done that with his own hands, with a poison he himself had made. He knew it was the only thing he could have done, and he didn't regret it because it meant that this demon hadn't died in as much pain as she would have if he hadn't done anything, but it still tore his heart out.

He moved to the side just in time to throw up. His stomach heaved. He was relieved he hadn't had breakfast this morning. There wasn't much for him to throw up, and it hurt his stomach and throat, but he didn't care. He felt like, in a way, he deserved to feel this pain.

"Everything all right, healer?" someone asked.

Reyni looked up to find a guard staring down at him. He didn't recognize the demon, but when they offered him a hand, he took it and allowed them to haul him to his feet. His mouth tasted foul, and his hands were dirty with even more blood now.

"I'm fine," he said.

The demon glanced at the body of the dead demon. "I'm sorry you had to see that."

"I'm sorry she had to die."

"At least she wasn't alone."

Reyni hated those words, but they were true. If he had to die, he wouldn't want to die alone.

But it wasn't fair. She shouldn't have had to die at all.

* * * *

Things stayed the same initially. Mikal could hear people screaming in the distance, but most of it seemed to be far enough away from their wing of the palace. It was a relief, but at the same time, it made Mikal want to scream. He hated waiting, especially in this kind of situation.

He wasn't surprised when the fight moved toward them. He suspected that the reason the palace had been attacked was to get to Berith's family. If they got his consort and his daughter, they could use them against him. Mikal had no doubt that, eventually, they would be killed, but first, they'd be used to manipulate Berith.

Mikal wouldn't allow that to happen. He wouldn't fail his prince.

There was a scream from much closer than before. Everyone in the room jumped, and Mel pressed closer to Mikal.

"They're here," the guard in the hallway said.

"Keep them away from the door for as long as you can," Mikal ordered, even though he knew it was probably a death sentence.

"I will," the guard promised.

Mikal hoped they would survive. He hoped they all would and that he'd finally have the opportunity to thank the guard, whoever they were. He wasn't sure how he'd find them, but if they were still standing by the time this was over, he'd try to recruit them for Berith's guards.

"What's happening?" Mel asked. His voice was unsteady, and he was paler than Mikal had ever seen him.

Mikal wasn't going to lie to him or to anyone else in the room. "They're here. The guards outside the door will protect us for as long as possible, but there's a chance they'll manage to get in."

Mikal half expected Mel to start freaking out and screaming. Most people would have. That wasn't what Mel did, though. Instead of starting to cry, he squared his shoulders and nodded. "Tell us what to do," he said.

They were in the suite of rooms Berith shared with Mel. Mikal had chosen this place for a reason. There were multiple exits, but all of them were easily guarded, and, more importantly, some of them were hidden, including the secret passages that led out of the palace.

"I need you to go into the secret passage," he ordered. "Don't go far until I get there."

Mikal wished he could send them away, but there was no way to know what they would find on the other side of the passage, so he couldn't risk it. There was always a chance that he and the guards would manage to stop the people trying to get in, and it would be safer for the consort and the heir to stay here.

For now, anyway.

Thankfully, Mel didn't hesitate. He moved to the side of the bed he shared with Berith and pressed something on a decoration on the wall. The wall opened, and Mel looked back, possibly asking Mikal for permission. Mikal nodded, and Mel turned toward Aloise.

"I want to fight," Cyarea declared.

Mikal blinked down at her. She'd taken out something from her pocket, and he realized it was a butter knife. She'd probably stolen it from the breakfast table this morning.

Seeing her like this, ready to protect her mother and the rest of her family, made Mikal smile. They couldn't ask for a better princess, and she'd be a force to be reckoned with once she was on the throne, but she was so young now. She shouldn't have to live through any of this, and she certainly shouldn't have to defend herself and her mother from demons trying to kill her.

"That's my job," he said gently.

She narrowed her eyes at him. "I can fight. Daddy taught me."

Mel made a strangled sound. Mikal had no idea what was

going through his head, but he knew what he felt. He was sad that Cyarea had to do this but also proud. Hell was a hard place to be born and grow up in. It took humanity out of demons before they were even out of diapers. Cyarea had kept that humanity, and it had made her softer than a lot of demons, but she was still fierce. Frankly, it was a little scary to see her so ready to stab someone.

"Mel can't fight," Mikal said.

Mel glared at him, but he didn't say anything. He knew Mikal was right.

Cyarea cocked her head.

"If anyone gets to him, you can stab them with your knife," Mikal explained.

Cyarea took a moment to think about that. Mikal glanced toward the door, nodding at the two guards standing in front of it. They could all hear the fighting in the hallway, and Mikal knew they didn't have much time. They needed to be out of here before the door was broken down.

"I'll go with him," Cyarea finally said.

Mikal breathed a sigh of relief and gently pushed her toward Mel. Several things happened at once as he did so.

Cyarea stopped moving when something heavy hit the door. The two guards in front of it raised their swords, and the door splintered. Mel whimpered, and Cyarea quickly placed herself in front of him, raising her butter knife.

Mikal didn't have the time to take care of Mel and Cyarea. He took out his sword and nodded at Aloise, who had two knives in her hands and was trying to usher Cyarea and Mel into the passage. She might not be as good a fighter as Mikal, but she'd protect Mel and Cyarea. Mikal trusted her to have their backs.

Then the door caved in.

Chapter Fourteen

Reyni wasn't sure how he'd ended up here. He'd been going from wounded demon to wounded demon, trying to help as many of them as he could, and now, he was so far down the enemy army that he could see Jessamyn from where he'd crouched.

He'd been trying to help a demon who'd had his leg torn off. Unfortunately, the demon had died before Reyni could do anything to help him, and he'd been about to move on to someone else when he heard someone scream. He'd looked up, and there Jessamyn was.

Reyni had never met her, but it could only be her. Unlike everyone else on the battlefield, she wasn't bloody or sweaty. She was wearing a white, flowing gown, something no one else would even think of wearing during a battle. Between the white and the jewelry, it was clear she wanted to set herself apart. She wasn't one to fight her own battles. Instead, she expected others to do it for her, and they had.

Reyni pressed his hand against the ground so he wouldn't fall on his face. He grimaced when his palm touched down. Blood had soaked into the dirt, turning it into mud. Reyni wasn't sure he'd ever be able to get the smell out of his nose.

He needed to go back. He was too close to Jessamyn and her army than he was comfortable with, and he was starting to panic. So far, they hadn't noticed him, maybe because he wore all black or maybe because he was half-hidden between the bodies, but even though he wanted to help more people, he wanted to live even more. That meant going back to Berith.

He glanced back. Berith wasn't far. Reyni could see him from where he was, too, so really, the only thing he had to do was to sneak away.

That was easier said than done.

He moved slowly and tried to stay down, but it wasn't easy. His legs hurt, and he kept stumbling on dead bodies and abandoned weapons. He continued moving forward because he didn't have a choice, but it was slow going, so much so that when he turned around, he could still see Jessamyn clearly.

That meant he could also see Lucifer when he suddenly appeared there. Reyni had no idea where he'd come from, but he watched with wide eyes as the demon stood in front of his sister.

Jessamyn screamed. Reyni didn't know if it was because she was surprised to see Lucifer or because she was afraid of him. If he had to guess, it was both.

"I didn't think you'd be this stupid," Lucifer drawled as he glanced around.

His sister's guards stepped forward, but he didn't seem intimidated, not even when she yelled at them to attack him. They obeyed, and Reyni closed his eyes when Lucifer moved toward them.

He didn't blame Lucifer for defending himself, and he wouldn't blame him for killing Jessamyn, but that didn't mean he wanted to see it. He already knew what needed to be done, and by now, he also knew that his heart was too soft. He'd sleep better if he didn't see the details of what was going on — if he ever slept again. He was sure he'd have nightmares.

The sound of bodies dropping to the ground told him he could open his eyes again. Lucifer was still standing, still looking as neat and handsome as if he hadn't just killed a bunch of demons. He wore black, so even if he'd gotten blood on his clothes, Reyni couldn't see it.

"Really?" Lucifer asked his sister. "You thought this would be enough?" Lucifer opened his arms. "You brought all these demons to their death, and for what? What did you think you'd obtain?"

"You stole my throne," Jessamyn said as she squared her shoulders.

It looked like she was trying to make herself look taller, but next to Lucifer, it was useless. Not only was he taller than her, but his presence was stronger. They were both intimidating and scary, but one of them was scarier, and it wasn't Jessamyn.

"I know humans view the underworld as a real version of their Hell, but that doesn't mean you have to work so hard to make it so," Lucifer said nonchalantly. "This place is harsh enough as it is. It doesn't need you on the throne. You would turn the underworld into a world of blood and pain, and there's already enough of that to go around already. Give it up, Jessamyn. You'll never have the throne. I won't let you anywhere near it."

She screeched and reached for her waist. With her flowy clothes, Reyni hadn't noticed that she was armed. He should have expected it. Everyone else probably had.

Lucifer certainly had. When Jessamyn threw herself at him, he smoothly moved out of the way, still smiling. She raised two knives and turned, slashing at him.

Reyni sucked in a breath. He hadn't planned on having to take care of Lucifer, of all people, today. He would if Lucifer needed him, but the demon was intimidating, and Reyni would feel more comfortable staying far away from him. He wanted to know what was going on, but he wanted to be at a safe distance from the fighting more, so he continued moving back. Most demons in the area were either busy killing each other or watching the fight between Lucifer and Jessamyn, so they didn't bother him. He was grateful because it meant he managed to reach Berith without getting hurt or having to stop.

Lon grabbed Reyni's shoulder and squeezed. "Where have you been?"

"Around."

Lon rolled his eyes. "Of course you have. You couldn't help yourself, could you?"

"People needed me."

"Mikal needs you more than anyone here. I'm sorry to say that, but it's true."

"I'm fine."

Lon stared at Reyni for a moment before nodding. "I'll take your word for that."

Reyni turned back to Lucifer, who had his sister pinned on the ground. Her white gown wasn't so white anymore. Lucifer was pressing her into the ground with his foot on her stomach, and she was trying to stab his leg to get free. Reyni winced when one of the knives penetrated Lucifer's calf, but Lucifer barely reacted. He wrinkled his nose, then leaned down and grabbed his sister by the throat. He hauled her up, raising her body so that everyone around them could see her.

Reyni averted his eyes. He understood why Lucifer was making a spectacle, and he didn't blame him, especially if it stopped the fighting, but he still didn't like any of this.

"You attacked my ally," Lucifer's voice boomed around the battlefield. "More than an ally, Berith is a friend, and you knew that, yet you still attacked him."

Jessamyn glared at him. She didn't say anything. She probably knew that it would be useless and that whatever came out of her mouth, she was about to die. Screaming wouldn't help her. Begging wouldn't do anything. She was dead, even though her heart was still beating.

Lucifer glanced around at the demons staring at them. It

was like everyone on the battlefield was holding their breath. Reyni certainly was.

"You chose the wrong side," Lucifer told the observers. "You now have a choice. You can continue fighting for my sister and Ramiel and die doing so, or you can leave and not look back. I won't try to stop you. I won't kill you. You'll be able to leave and heal and maybe build yourself a life. I won't hold your presence here against you."

Reyni was glad he was back with Berith and Lon. It would have been scary to still be on the other side, where the demons were dropping their weapons and running away as fast as they could, mowing down anyone who stood in their way. He leaned closer to Lon, who squeezed his shoulder again. He hadn't let go yet.

Lucifer turned to Jessamyn. "Any last words?" he asked.

When she spoke, it was too softly for Reyni to hear what she was saying. Lucifer did, though. He didn't have any reaction. His expression didn't change. He leaned closer to listen to his sister, then back.

He dropped her. She dove for something on the ground, probably a weapon. She never got there. A sword appeared in Lucifer's hand. He slashed at her, and for a second, everything was still and quiet. Then, Jessamyn's body slumped on the ground, her head sliding away from her neck. Reyni sucked in a breath and looked away.

He didn't feel sorry for her. He just didn't want to see that. She and Ramiel's demons wouldn't be dead if it weren't for her foolishness and her belief that she could take her brother on in a fight for the throne. She'd gotten what she deserved. She'd known this would end like this if she lost, and she had.

A loud explosion made Reyni jump. He turned, his eyes widening in horror when he saw smoke coming from the palace.

Lon swore and turned to Berith. Neither of them said

anything. They moved as one, running toward the palace. Reyni ran after them.

CHAPTER FIFTEEN

When two demons rushed inside, Mikal was ready for them. He could hear more fighting outside the door, a sure sign that not all the guards had been killed or incapacitated. He couldn't worry about them right now, though. The only thing he needed to worry about was protecting Berith's family, and that was what he did.

He met the first demon with his sword. It sank into the demon's thigh, and when Mikal pulled it out and swung it again, into the demon's neck this time.

He turned to the second attacker before the first body dropped to the floor.

The demon was reaching for Mel. Mel's eyes were wide, and he was pressing back against the wall, but he wasn't running away. Mikal swore and moved, but before he could get there, the demon screamed and stumbled back. Mikal looked down just in time to see Cyarea pull her butter knife out of the demon's leg and stab him again.

He almost laughed. The only reason he didn't was that the demon was reaching for her, and Mikal would rather die than allow him to touch her. He grabbed the demon's arm and pulled him back, hooking his foot around the demon's ankle to make him fall. If the demon happened to fall right on Mikal's sword, it wasn't Mikal's fault.

"I wanted to kill him," Cyarea declared.

Mikal rolled his eyes and gestured at her mother to take

her. It took a bit of convincing, but once Mel got involved, too, the three of them disappeared into the secret passage. Mikal quickly closed it behind them. He could hear them just behind the wall, but they were out of sight, which meant he didn't have to worry about them as more demons poured in.

He lost himself in the fight. He didn't know how many demons he stabbed, beheaded, and tore apart. He didn't care, either. He just needed them to stop trying to get to Mel and Cyarea.

He got a cut on the cheek that made him wince because he knew what Reyni would have to say about it. His thigh ached, but it was nothing he couldn't ignore as he did his job.

He was still relieved when, after cutting off the hand of another demon, he straightened and got ready for the next attacker, but no one came.

Mikal panted as he glanced around the room. He grimaced because he knew Berith wouldn't be happy to see this many dead bodies in his bedroom, but it wasn't like Mikal had a choice. It was either that or allowing them to reach Mel.

A noise at the door made him turn. He raised his sword, ready to continue fighting, but he recognized the uniform of the guard who stumbled in before he could do irreversible damage.

The guard was clutching their arm against their chest. Part of their left ear was missing, and their hair was bloody, probably because of a head wound that ran all the way down their forehead. Their eyes were wide as they took in the room, but they relaxed, and Mikal allowed himself to do the same.

"Sorry, I couldn't help. I was busy out there," the guard said.

Mikal grinned. "You're the guard who warned us."

He was surprised to see that he and the guard shared the same light green skin, tusks, black hair, and horns. Mikal's were much smaller, but that didn't change anything. He and the guard were of the same species. It was a surprise because they didn't usually stray away from their people. They were born in their clan and died in their clan. They didn't work for anyone but their clan elders.

The guard dropped their arm and winced. "I am."

Mikal gestured at them to sit down on the bed. He thought the guard was male because of how long their horns were, but he didn't want to assume. A lot of people had assumed Mikal was female when he wasn't, and he wouldn't do that to anyone.

The guard eyed the bed and stayed on their feet until Mikal rolled his eyes and pushed them toward it. "Sit down. Mel and Berith won't care. I'm pretty sure they're going to have to burn everything that was in this room and get new furniture, anyway."

The guard finally relented. They were pale, and Mikal wouldn't have been surprised if they'd fainted if they hadn't sat down.

"Your name?" Mikal asked as he moved around the room, checking on the fallen demons and ensuring they were dead.

"Jalin"

Mikal nodded. A male, then. "Mikal."

"I don't think there's anyone in the palace who doesn't know who you are," Jalin said. "It was an honor to fight by your side."

Mikal snickered. "You were outside, not by my side. It was an honor to fight with you, though." He pressed his hand against the decoration on the wall to open the secret passage now that he was sure every attacker in the room was dead.

The wall popped open. Mikal expected Aloise to be first in line, but instead, he was greeted by Cyarea, who was still clutching her now bloody butter knife. She pouted when she saw it was him.

"I thought I'd get to stab another demon."

Her mother hauled her into her arms and rolled her eyes. "One fight and you turn all bloodthirsty. We're going to have to do something about that," she said as she walked her daughter out of the passage.

Mel was next. He was shaking and pale, but he didn't hesitate to come out. He stumbled when he first saw the room, but Mikal was there, holding him up and wrapping an arm around his shoulders. Normally, he wouldn't be nearly as familiar with the consort, but Mel needed support.

"Thank you," Mel whispered. "Do you think we can go to the dining room or something?"

"Of course. You're probably hungry."

Mel grimaced. "Not really. I just don't want to see this. I know it makes me weak, but it's too much."

Mikal squeezed Mel's shoulders. "It doesn't make you weak. It makes you sensitive and human."

Mel snorted. "That's what I am, so I guess it's a good thing." He looked at Jalin. "You helped Mikal?"

Jalin's eyes were wide as he nodded. "I did, Consort."

"Please, none of that. Call me Mel, and follow us to the dining room."

Jalin looked at Mikal as if asking for permission. Mikal shrugged. Mel was doing what Mel did best—making friends in the strangest places.

They left the bodies behind and headed to the dining room. They were still in the prince's private wing, but it wasn't as quiet and neat as usual. There were bodies everywhere and blood on the floor and walls. Mikal was relieved to see that only a few of the demons who'd been killed wore the guards' uniform. They'd lost people, but not nearly as many as they could have.

He wasn't surprised to see there were already people gathered in the dining room. He *was* surprised to see Bretton, Lucifer's assistant and best friend. He was fussing over Dimri, of all people.

"I'm fine," Dimri said with a grunt as he tried pulling away from Bretton.

"You're bleeding from your shoulder," Bretton pointed out.

"You're not a healer, so it's none of your business."

Mikal shook his head and helped Mel, Cyarea, and Aloise find empty seats. Mel had just sat down when the door swung open, slamming against the wall. Berith strode in, already looking around, and Mel shot out of his chair. Cyarea was right behind him.

Mikal relaxed. With Berith here, Mel was safe.

Lon and Roque came in after Berith. Mikal arched a brow when he saw that Roque made a beeline for Bretton and Dimri and started fussing over Dimri's wound, too. Mikal was curious, but he wasn't about to ask questions and make a fool of himself, especially when he noticed Reyni frantically looking around.

He was wearing black, so Mikal couldn't see the blood on his clothes, but he could smell it. He wanted to tear the clothes off Reyni's body and burn them, but instead, he cleared his throat and opened his arms. Reyni whimpered when he saw him and rushed forward, throwing himself against Mikal's chest. Mikal winced at the sensation of Reyni's clothes against him.

"Are you hurt?" Reyni asked, leaning back.

"I'm fine. We all are. Well, except for Jalin, so you should probably check in on him. He helped us fight off the demons who attacked us in Mel's bedroom."

Reyni nodded, but he didn't move away. Mikal was glad because he wasn't quite ready to let him go.

It would be a long time before he could do so without being afraid that something would happen to the demon he loved.

* * * *

Reyni knew he needed to go to Mel and Cyarea and check them over. They were his priority since he was the prince's healer. He also needed to check in on this Jalin that Mikal had mentioned and, of course, make sure that Mikal was fine.

But Reyni couldn't move. He couldn't step away from Mikal. He was terrified that if he did, something would happen. It was a miracle that both of them were alive. Reyni hadn't dared hope this would happen, and now that it had, he wanted to cry.

Luckily for him, he wasn't the only healer in the room. He wasn't surprised to see two of his apprentices bustling in carrying bandages and other supplies they would need. Reyni didn't even need to order them around. They went straight to work.

"Everyone, sit down," Berith ordered.

Reyni was happy to obey. His legs felt like jelly. He wasn't on the battlefield anymore, and the adrenaline was leaving his system. His hands shook as he flopped into the closest chair, letting go of Mikal only for a few seconds before grabbing his hand again. Mikal pushed their chairs together and wrapped an arm around Reyni's shoulders, holding him close.

"What's the situation like in the palace?" Berith asked as he turned to Lon, who had his phone in his hand.

"Uri confirmed that all enemy demons have been neutralized. Clean-up hasn't started yet, and we lost some guards, but all in all, it seems to have gone better than we expected.

"The servants?"

"I have news of a few casualties, but most of them seem to have been ignored. The attackers were looking for your family. They only killed the demons who stood in their way."

Berith nodded and finally sat down. No one was surprised

when he pulled Mel into his lap. For once, Mel didn't appear embarrassed at the thought of cuddling in front of other people. He snuggled right in, looking like he was nowhere near ready to let go of Berith. Reyni understood that. He wasn't ready to let go of Mikal, either.

He might never be.

He closed his eyes. He'd never been quite this exhausted, so he wasn't surprised that when he opened them after what felt like only a few seconds later, he realized that it had been longer. Servants were coming in, carrying food and more supplies for the apprentices, who were still moving around the room. Reyni blinked and sat up, knowing he needed to help them, but Berith caught his eye and shook his head. He tilted his chin at the food on the table, and even though Reyni had been sure he'd ever be able to eat again just half an hour ago, now, he was starving.

He grabbed a piece of bread and stuffed it into his mouth, moaning at the taste. Mikal made a strangled sound, but Reyni didn't stop to wonder about it. He was too hungry, and he had work to do.

Guards moved in and out of the room, reporting to Lon and Berith. As soon as Reyni felt he wasn't about to starve, he got up and went to work, too. Mikal had mentioned Jalin, so Reyni went to him first. The demon looked remarkably like Mikal. He was holding his arm and sitting at the end of the table as if he was ready to bolt.

Reyni grabbed one of the bags containing the supplies he'd need and went to sit next to Jalin. Jalin stared at him with wide eyes.

"I know the feeling," Reyni said as he gently touched Jalin's arm. "You have no idea what you're doing here. You feel like you shouldn't be because this is the prince's family."

Jalin nodded. "How do you know?"

"I felt the same just a few weeks ago. Even Mikal felt that

way initially."

Jalin glanced at Mikal, who was talking to Lon and Berith. Their expressions were serious. "But *he* belongs here."

"Does he? You're the same species, right?"

Jalin nodded. "Yeah. It's why I volunteered to warn him that we were under attack. We don't usually leave our clans, and I'd heard things about him."

"Things about his horns?" Reyni asked as he poked at the wound in Jalin's arm.

Jalin winced. "I know what I heard, and I know what I saw. Whatever the length of his horns, he's an excellent fighter. He wouldn't be protecting the prince's family if he wasn't."

Reyni nodded, satisfied. He didn't know if Mikal missed his clan, but if he did, having Jalin here could help. At the very least, it didn't sound like it would do any damage since Jalin seemed to admire Mikal.

"Well, if I have to guess, I think you're about to become part of his family, too," he told Jalin. "It'll take some time to get used to, but you won't find a better group of people. Berith isn't just a prince. He cares about all of us, and once you become part of his family, he treats you as such."

"I'm not part of his family," Jalin whispered.

"You helped Mikal. You protected Mel, Cyarea, and Aloise. That's enough for Berith to take you in."

Jalin looked like he might run away at the suggestion, but Reyni forced him to stay. Once he was done cleaning and stitching the wound in Jalin's arm, he put a plate together so that Jalin could eat. He was still at the edge of the table, away from everyone else, but he was there.

Reyni didn't miss the way Berith nodded at him when he saw what he was doing. There would be a conversation with Berith in Jalin's future, but Reyni didn't say anything about that for now. He wouldn't want Jalin to freak out and run screaming for the hills.

Reyni checked everyone in the room, even Bretton, who glared at him and insisted he hadn't been anywhere near the fighting. Only once Reyni was satisfied that no one was about to die did he sit back next to Mikal, feeling even more exhausted than before. He needed his bed, possibly with Mikal in it, but from the way Mikal was talking to Lon and Berith, Reyni suspected he'd have to go home alone tonight. Everyone had a lot of work to do, but the work for Berith, Lon, Mikal, and the guards was the most important.

They'd need to protect the palace and its inhabitants. The battle had been won, but it wasn't over. Ramiel was still out there, aiming for Berith's throne. He'd have to take a break, but that didn't mean he would vanish entirely. If anything, he'd probably return with even more demons.

Reyni leaned against Mikal's side. Mikal instantly wrapped an arm around him without even looking at him. The gesture made Reyni smile.

"Where's Lucifer?" he asked no one in particular. Lucifer had been wounded, but Reyni hadn't yet checked him over.

"He stayed back to glare at the few demons who stuck around after he killed Jessamyn," Lon explained. "He wanted to be sure they wouldn't attack the palace while we were here."

"They'll leave if they know what's good for them. I'm pretty sure Lucifer could kill them with a thought."

Mikal snorted. "I know you probably don't want to talk about it, but I'm curious about what happened out there."

He was right. Reyni did *not* want to talk about anything he'd seen today. In fact, he hoped to be able to forget every single detail.

He wouldn't be able to. Maybe talking about it would help, and maybe it wouldn't. He wouldn't keep anything from Mikal, though. If Mikal wanted to know, Reyni would tell him.

But not today. Today, he'd have more food, drag himself to his rooms, take a bath, and fall into bed. He wouldn't be any good to his patients in the state he was in, which meant he needed to get some rest before getting back to the infirmary.

But not yet. For now, he was happy to snuggle against Mikal and close his eyes.

* * * *

Mikal had thought it would be near impossible for him to relax after everything that had happened, but he'd been wrong. Part of it was exhaustion, but another part was having his friends and family around him.

They'd survived. They'd all survived, from Berith to Lon to Reyni. Mikal almost couldn't believe he hadn't lost anyone.

The fight wasn't over yet. It would be a while before it was, depending on whether or not they could get their hands on Ramiel, but if Mikal had to guess, the demon would go into hiding until he could rebuild his army. He'd lost a lot of fighters, and he wasn't stupid. If he wanted to win his fight against Berith, he was going to need a lot of manpower. Lucifer had shown everyone that he was on Berith's side and wouldn't hesitate to kill to defend Berith and his territory. That would give many demons pause because they'd seen how powerful Lucifer was now. He'd killed his sister without hesitation.

It didn't take long for everyone in the room to leave. They all needed sleep, and Mikal suspected that Berith wanted to check in on Mel himself. Mel was fine — he didn't even have a scratch — but Mikal understood. Berith needed to see that with his own two eyes to reassure himself.

"I wanted to thank you," Berith quietly said when Mikal walked up to him to promise he'd have his report by tomorrow morning.

"I did my job," Mikal answered.

"Yes, you did, and you did it well. I know that you would have sacrificed your own life to save Mel's, whether or not it was your job. That means a lot to me. You kept him and the rest of my family safe, including my daughter when she decided to start stabbing people."

Mikal snickered. Cyarea had fallen asleep in her mother's arms about half an hour ago, and she looked like an innocent angel, even with the butter knife still clutched in her hand. Mikal knew she was anything but. He'd seen her stab a demon with that knife. "Well, she made sure to tell me that you taught her how to fight."

"I did. I just never thought she'd have to put it into practice."

"I know you try to shelter her, and you're doing a good job allowing her to grow up as simply and happily as possible, but we live in the underworld. Eventually, she's going to realize what that means, and she'll be grateful that you taught her how to defend herself and the people she loves."

Berith glanced at his daughter. "She'll be a good ruler."

"She will be, as long as she manages to get her stabbing habit under control."

For a moment, Mikal wondered if he'd pushed too far. He and Berith were friends, but Berith was also Mikal's prince, and Mikal was talking about his daughter. Berith smiled, though, allowing Mikal to relax again. His head was safely on his shoulders.

"Take Reyni home," Berith said. "We all need rest, and if I know him, he'll be back in the infirmary tomorrow morning before the sun rises."

"He has a lot of work to do. We all do."

Berith nodded. "The fight isn't over, unfortunately."

It wasn't, but they'd won the first battle, and that meant

something.

When Mikal returned to Reyni after quickly talking to Lon, too, he found him with Jalin. Jalin looked overwhelmed and kept eyeing the door, but he was also nodding at whatever Reyni was saying. Reyni gestured with his hands as he spoke, almost smacking down a glass on the table. Mikal's heart squeezed at the sight. He could have lost this. He could have lost Reyni.

When Reyni heard Mikal coming behind him, he tilted his head up and smiled at him.

It was like coming home. Reyni was Mikal's. He wanted him, had *chosen* him, something no one else had ever done. How was Mikal supposed to resist?

He wasn't, and he didn't want to.

"Ready to go home?" Mikal asked.

Reyni looked like he might cry. "Yes, please. These clothes are disgusting. I can't believe I actually ate food wearing them. They smell awful and feel even worse, which I didn't think was possible."

"We were hungry. Come on. You can take a bath and put on something comfortable to sleep in. Your work will still be here tomorrow." And so would Reyni.

"Do you need anything?" Reyni asked as he turned to Jalin. "I can ask someone to walk you back to your room."

Jalin shot to his feet, clearly ready to leave. He probably would have left as soon as Berith had entered the room if he'd been able to. "I'll be fine. It's just my arm, and you patched me up."

"Well, you lost quite a bit of blood, so make sure to have breakfast tomorrow and sleep as much as you can tonight. Lon will put you back to work as soon as he can, but if you have any pain or stiffness, come to the infirmary. I'll take care of you."

"Thank you," Jalin said. He sounded overwhelmed but

also like he meant it.

Mikal was curious to find out why Jalin had left his clan. Usually, their species didn't. Mikal had left because it was the only way for him to live his own life and to get away from a clan that thought less of him because of his horns, but what was Jalin's story? Mikal wasn't about to ask. Maybe Jalin would share with him one day. In the meantime, Mikal would keep an eye on him. They might not be related or belong to the same clan, but it meant something to have Jalin here. Besides, Mikal had thought Jalin was doing a great job even before he'd realized they were the same species. At the very least, Jalin deserved a raise and promotion for his help in protecting Mel and the rest of Berith's family.

"Come to my office tomorrow," he told Jalin. "Whenever you have time. We'll both be busy, so don't be surprised if you don't find me there, but I'd like to talk to you."

Jalin nodded stiffly. "Of course."

"Good."

Jalin almost ran out of the room. In fact, he was moving so quickly that he stumbled out the door and had to catch himself on the wall. Mikal chuckled and shook his head. He had enough work keeping Reyni safe, mostly from himself. Was he going to have to do the same for Jalin?

"I like him," Reyni said.

"Yeah?"

"Well, he helped you fight those demons, so of course I was going to like him, but he's also nice."

"I haven't talked to him much, but I agree. Ready to go home?"

"I was ready an hour ago."

Everyone looked like they were about to fall asleep where they stood, so Mikal didn't hesitate to drag Reyni out of the dining room. They made their way down the hallways to Reyni's rooms. Mikal kept an eye open, just in case, but the only enemy demons they saw were dead ones. Servants and guards were already dragging out the bodies and cleaning the floors and walls, but it would take some time to get everything back to normal.

Maybe they never would. After all, Ramiel was still out there, waiting for his time to fight. Mikal wanted to hope he'd see this was a bad idea and take a step back, but Mikal doubted they'd be that lucky.

Reyni started stripping as soon as they entered his rooms. He didn't even wait until he was in the bathroom. He shed his black uniform right there by the front door, then rushed away, leaving everything there. Mikal doubted Reyni would ever want to see these clothes again, so he bundled them up and dropped them outside the door. Someone would either clean them or burn them. It didn't matter, although Mikal doubted that anyone could get the fabric clean again. It was stiff with drying blood. The thought of Reyni and everything he'd gone through while wearing his clothes made Mikal want to scream.

He wanted to rage against Jessamyn and Ramiel. He wanted to hurt them for all the pain they were causing. Jessamyn was dead, so he wouldn't get the chance to do that, but Ramiel wasn't. Maybe Mikal would have a chance at revenge, eventually.

But revenge wasn't what he wanted to think about today. He abandoned his clothes by the bathroom door and walked in fully naked. He didn't miss the way Reyni carefully avoided staring at him, but he ignored it. They both needed to clean up, and the bathtub was full. Besides, they'd spent last night together. They might not have had sex, and they probably wouldn't tonight, either — Mikal doubted he'd have the energy to do more than kiss Reyni good night — but they were in this for the long term, and he'd never been ashamed of the way he looked.

He quickly showered off the grime and blood from his body. When he moved toward the tub, Reyni made to get up, but Mikal slid behind him and pulled him back down. Reyni squeaked, making Mikal laugh and wish he'd have more energy. Unfortunately for him, his eyes were already sliding close.

"We should go to bed," Reyni said as Mikal guided him to lean his back against Mikal's chest.

Mikal's back was against the edge of the tub, and it was cold, but it felt good. It especially felt good to have Reyni between his legs like this. Mikal's body tried, it really did, but he just couldn't get hard. He didn't have enough energy left.

"Soon," Mikal murmured.

"We better because if we don't, we'll fall asleep in the tub and drown."

Mikal squeezed his arms around Reyni. "Don't be so negative. We survived the battle. I'm sure we can survive a bath, too."

Reyni turned his head and kissed Mikal's cheek. "We have to because I have plans for you tomorrow morning."

Mikal's eyes were shut so he couldn't see Reyni's expression, but he could imagine it. It made him smile. "Oh?"

"And you won't find out what those plans are unless we get into bed."

If Mikal had ever needed an incentive to get cleaned up, this was it.

EPILOGUE

When Mikal woke up, he might as well have been in heaven. He was in Reyni's bed, flat on his back, with an arm around Reyni's shoulders. Reyni was snuggled against him, his cheek pressed to Mikal's chest, one of his legs slung on top of Mikal's thighs. He clung to Mikal as if he was afraid Mikal would vanish during the night, but Mikal wasn't going anywhere.

He was planning on spending the rest of his life here. It might be too fast for most people, but he didn't need more time. He'd been in love with Reyni for months, even before they'd gotten together. They should have spoken sooner, but this was good, too. They'd gotten to know each other as friends, and now, they could slide into a relationship as easily as breathing.

Mikal leaned down to kiss the top of Reyni's head. Reyni snuffled and pressed his nose harder against Mikal's chest. Mikal turned to stare at the ceiling, wondering how long they could get away with staying in bed. He couldn't stop smiling.

He was surprised no one had tried waking them up yet. He could hear people moving around the palace, and he knew how much work there was to do. Reyni would want to check the infirmary and every new patient he'd gained during the battle. Mikal needed to find Yuri and go over how many guards they had left. Berith and his family were a priority, so

Mikal might have to pull people from the palace guard, but that shouldn't be a problem. He doubted he would even have to talk to Lon about it. Lon knew that Mikal had everything in hand, which meant he could focus on staying by Berith's side and deal with whatever Ramiel would throw at them next.

"It's too early," Reyni mumbled.

"I don't know about that. The sun is already up."

"Doesn't mean anything. I'm still tired."

Mikal suspected they would all still be tired one week from now, but there was no way out of it. They needed to clean the palace and rebuild the part that had been blown up. They needed to train and be ready for when Ramiel would attack. Unfortunately, they couldn't do that from the bed.

"Don't you want to go and check in on your new patients?" he asked Reyni.

Reyni tilted his head up and blinked hard. "Why are you talking about work? We're in bed together, completely naked."

Mikal grinned. "Right. You did promise me something yesterday."

Reyni still looked half-asleep, but he'd never been more beautiful. "Did I? Maybe you should remind me of that because I don't think I remember," Reyni teased.

Mikal rolled until they were both on their sides facing each other. Reyni's leg was still hooked around Mikal's thigh, but Mikal grabbed it and slid it higher until it was around his waist. They were pressed together, breathing the same air, and Mikal couldn't believe how lucky he was. He leaned closer to kiss Reyni.

Someone knocked on the door.

Mikal groaned, and Reyni looked ready to scream. Instead, he turned to glare at the door. "What?"

There was a pause before someone answered. "I'm really

sorry to bother you, Healer Reyni, but the prince is looking for Mikal."

Mikal grabbed his pillow and pushed his head under it. Maybe he could hide.

"What does the prince want?" Reyni asked.

"For Mikal to go to his office as soon as possible. Lucifer is here."

Unfortunately, there would be no hiding for Mikal. He couldn't exactly tell the king of Hell that he'd rather spend the morning in bed with his lover than talk to him. It wasn't even that he thought that Lucifer would be offended. If anything, he'd be amused and agree. But whatever was happening had to be related to what had happened yesterday, and Berith wouldn't want Mikal there if it weren't necessary.

He pushed the pillow away and sat up, unfortunately dislodging Reyni from his body. "I have to go."

"I'm going to yell at Lucifer the next time I see him," Reyni growled.

"No, you won't," Mikal said as he quickly kissed Reyni before getting to his feet. "You're just as eager to get to your infirmary as I am to find out what's going on. Besides, the sooner we solve all of this, the sooner we can start living in peace again."

"I do have a lot of work," Reyni murmured.

Knowing him, he was already thinking about how to organize the infirmary so that he could keep an eye on everyone. Mikal had no doubt that Reyni's mother was already hard at work, and Reyni would join her as soon as Mikal was out the door.

Mikal didn't know when he and Reyni would see each other again today, so after getting dressed in clothes brought up by a servant, he paused by the bed. He knelt next to Reyni, who had wrapped himself in the blanket and was typing on his tablet.

"I'll see you tonight?" he murmured as he pulled Reyni into his arms.

Reyni didn't let go of the tablet, but he did look up long enough to kiss Mikal. "Not for lunch?"

"It depends if both of us are free for lunch. We can try."

Reyni nodded. "Please. Waiting until dinner to see you again would be too long."

"Someone has a crush," Mikal gently teased.

"If you haven't realized that by now, I'm doing a good job hiding my feelings."

"I don't want you to hide your feelings, not from me." Mikal kissed Reyni again, then forced himself to move away. "In fact, I want to know every single thing you're feeling."

"Right now, I'm annoyed and angry."

"I'll make sure to tell Berith that."

"Please do. He won't be surprised."

He definitely wouldn't. He knew Reyni.

Unfortunately, Mikal couldn't stay. It was hard to leave Reyni, but once he wasn't in front of Mikal, it was easier to focus on the day ahead of him. Mikal already had a mental list of everything he needed to know by the time he reached Berith's office.

He wasn't surprised to see that Lon was there. Dimri was sitting by the window, munching on a pastry and drinking coffee. There was a spread of food on the desk, and since Mikal hadn't stopped to have breakfast, he made a beeline for it, ignoring everyone until he had food and coffee.

"Nice of you to join us," Berith said with a grin.

"I can't imagine it was any easier for you to leave Mel than it was for me to leave Reyni."

Berith laughed. "You're right. I would still be with him if Lucifer hadn't decided he needed to talk to me."

Lucifer's smile was wicked and slightly worrying. Mikal was glad the king of Hell wasn't an enemy.

He was especially glad when Lucifer exposed his fangs. "I'm done waiting to be attacked. We allowed Jessamyn to come too close to us and our loved ones, but I won't make the same mistake when it comes to Ramiel. We're going to kill him and squash the rebellion. We'll take the fight to him instead of waiting for him to bring it to us."

Mikal sighed and leaned back against the desk. This was going to be a long day.

ABOUT THE AUTHOR

Catherine is the creator of several series, most of them paranormal, including the Whitedell Pride Series and the Gillham Pack Series. While she graduated in translation, she decided to go the writer's way because it was more fun to create her own stories and characters.

She lived in Italy for twenty-six years but has now returned home to the north of Europe.

She loves pizza—probably too much—her son, her pets, and, of course, books. She sneaks some reading time into her schedule every time she has five minutes free from writing, demands from her various pets and son, and lastly, housework.

www.ingramcontent.com/pod-product-compliance
Lightning Source LLC
Chambersburg PA
CBHW051250170626
46809CB00004B/1589